TREASURES FROM AFAR

Books by Troy D. Wymer

Lightyears Trilogy
Lightyears
Lightyears II: Intragalactic Terrorism
Lightyears III: Ominous Intervention

Treasures From Afar

Xeno Tryst Duology
Xeno Tryst
Feathers of Shardaa

Crystal Avarice

Treasures From Afar

Troy D. Wymer

This novel contains some sexual content and is intended for mature audiences.

WymerNovels, the "Atheneum of the Mind" tag line, and books logo are trademarks ™ by Troy D. Wymer

Published by WymerNovels

www.WymerNovels.com

ISBN: 979-8-9916986-1-0

Second Edition: 2025, Version 2.0

Published in the United States

Preface

I began writing *Treasures From Afar* in April 1991 on my new word processor. I settled into a more structured, plotter-style of writing than previously done on the *Lightyears Trilogy*. I finished the novel in March 1992. I was very pleased with the outcome of *Treasures From Afar.*

The original manuscript was stored on obsolete 3 inch proprietary disks. In 2011, I sent for these to be converted and had text files sent to me in return. It took me two years, but in 2018, I completed the revisions to my original manuscript, which has added some great improvements to the story.

Appendices are located at the end of this book with a chronology of emperors and empresses of the Imperium and a terminology glossary.

—Troy D. Wymer
October 24, 2025

Chapter One

Selnaan's annual historical art festival was being celebrated in the old city of Feenith. Valuable art and historical items were being sold, traded, and displayed. It was the festival's twenty-seventh anniversary. There was something special this time. It seemed to be more crowded. More people seemed to be interested in the occasion. Most people came to the festival just to observe and admire the art. However, art collectors came from around the galaxy to add to their collections from the vast array of art throughout the festival. It was evident that culture and history played a large role in the festival. As usual, there were Galactic Government Troops scattered throughout the area. They were watching the people to make sure they did not break any of the government's so-called laws.

The weather was just right. Beautiful sunshine brightened the day. The green fields surrounding Feenith danced as the winds blew through the tall grass. The fresh scent of spring was carried in the wind as it blew in toward the festival.

A man scanned his eyes across an array of ancient printing equipment. He slowly walked along an aisle. His attention was drawn across the aisle to a display of books on the other side. There were books from famous writers and poets. There were journals and encyclopedias of various types. He picked up a small book of poems.

"How much for this?" he asked the man behind the table.

"Five credits," the man said.

Shane grabbed his wallet from his back pocket and took out his digital currency card. He passed it through the scanner slot attached to the table and punched in his account number.

"Thank you," the man behind the table said.

Shane put the small book in his back pocket. He noticed a few government troops talking near a display of historical documents. He listened to their conversation. Soon, they left the immediate area. Then Shane walked over to the table.

"What was that all about?" Shane asked the woman behind the display.

"I guess they have orders to search for a missing historical document. Whatever it is, it seems to be urgent," the woman said.

"Oh, that's interesting," Shane said.

Shane looked through the documents on display at the woman's table. Most of them were old command notes from the First Tiffan Siram Empire. After examining them, he walked to a secluded area and looked around at all the people. An old man walked up to him.

"I noticed that you were inspecting those ancient empire notes."

"Yeah. Those types of things interest me. I remember when I was in college, I took a class on ancient documents," Shane said.

"Did you? I'm happy to see that I'm not the only one who is interested in that type of thing. You've also gone to college? Do you like adventure?" the old man asked.

"Well, that all depends."

"See this nice piece of art?" the man asked, holding up a painting of a beautiful animal running through a stream of water.

"Yeah."

"There is something hidden on the inside of the picture. You probably heard the government troops talking about it over there. The document they are searching for is in the back of this picture. It gives clues that lead to something wonderful. If I was your age, I would do it myself. But I want you to take it and get out of here. The troops are after me. Take the picture and go. Do you have a ship?"

"Yes."

"Then, take the picture and go. It leads to a treasure," the man said.

"A treasure?"

"Yes. Now, hurry!"

"Okay," Shane said, "if you think it's that important."

"I do. I do," the man said, looking over his shoulder.

Shane left the festival and headed for his ship. When he was inside the ship, he opened the back of the picture with a knife. The old cloth that covered the back of the picture cut away very easily. An ancient scroll rolled out of the picture and onto the ship floor. Just as Shane went to pick it up, there was a knock at his ship door. The sound echoed through the ship's hull. He walked back to see who was there.

"I am a Galactic Government official. From the markings on your ship, I take it that you are Shane Aslat?"

"Yes."

"You were seen with an older man earlier. He gave you an art piece. I want the art piece, now. It contains something that the government has been searching for, for quite some time."

Shane's mind raced for something to say. He really wanted to see what that treasure was all about. Why would the government be that interested in a scroll? Shane slammed the ship door and ran to the controls. He quickly started the ship and lifted from the surface of Selnaan.

Ariel stood in a doorway looking out into the rain. She wished that it would stop raining so she could do some business. There were not many people out in the rain. She looked up in the sky. The grayish sky was twisted with black drifts of clouds. The rain beat upon the sidewalk with its dancing drops. It had its own music. If one was to listen closely, they would hear it. Ariel heard it. She stared into the street. Most of the buildings around the area were abandoned. She noticed a bald man walking down the sidewalk toward her. She grew a smile and stepped out in front of him.

"How 'bout a little action, babe," she said, ripping her skirt half open.

"In exchange for what?" the man asked, looking at the rip in her skirt.

"What ya got?"

"Right now, I don't have anything that you would want."

"Then, what did you stop for?"

"You stepped out in front of me."

"Oh, get out of here."

Ariel stepped back into the doorway. The man resumed walking.

Why am I here on this dreadful planet? she thought.

She sat down on the ground in the doorway where it was dry and put her arms on her knees. She rested her head on her arms. When the rain slowed to a slight sprinkle, she got back to her feet and looked back out into the street. Was it going to be another day with no business? She dismissed the question as she saw the man that passed by a few minutes earlier coming back down the sidewalk toward her with a bag in his hand. He stopped where she stood.

"How about some action in exchange for lunch?"

Ariel looked at the bag of food. Her stomach growled.

"All right. Let's get to it."

"I'm in a hurry. Why don't we just go in this abandoned building here?"

"Whatever you want," she said, opening the door beside her.

They entered the building.

The rain was cold and damp as it fell on Shane while he ran through an alley. His boots were soaked from splashing through the puddles in his way. Not far behind him were several uniformed men with rifles. Shane dashed around a corner into another alley just as the men shot their laser rifles. Light blue beams of intense power destroyed an old brick wall. Shane's heart was pounding fiercely. Before the uniformed men ran around the corner, Shane went through a door into an old building. He noticed an old, wooden barrel hidden underneath a stairway. He quickly jumped inside and covered it with the lid. Soon, the door slammed open and the men entered. They looked around the room with a flashlight and then went up the stairs. After quite some time, the men came back down the stairs and left the building. When Shane felt that it was safe, he lifted the lid from the barrel and leaped out. Standing in the darkness, he looked around the room. There was light shining from the top of the stairs. He reached the bottom of the stairs and looked up. Necessity more than curiosity forced him to go up. As he walked up the creaky, wooden stairs, he noticed a couple of large spiders on his jacket. With a quick yelp of terror, he backed against the wall and flung the spiders down the stairs. When he reached the second level, he was surprised to find that he was in an abandoned hotel. He looked around the building. In the rooms on each side of the corridor, there were old, torn mattresses and other furniture covered with dust. One particular room adjacent from the corridor was clean and organized.

I wonder who's been keeping this room nice and neat, Shane thought.

Shane entered the hotel room and shut the door. To the left of the bed there was a dresser with a large mirror attached to it. To the right of the bed there was a chair, a closet full of clothes, and a small bathroom. The bed had a white comforter and two fluffy pillows on it. It looked very comfortable to Shane. He was extremely exhausted from the chase. He lay down on the bed and fell asleep.

Shane Aslat was one point eight meters tall. He had long, brown hair and green eyes. He wore a long, dangling earring in his left ear. He was a very intelligent and organized man. Throughout his life, he had been through many painful experiences. Because of the painful experiences and memories of it all, Shane was a very cautious man. He was basically searching for his inner self, his inner feelings. He was a drifter.

Shane was born on the planet Elbi and raised in a poor family. His parents were killed on Elbi in a series of wars, the Telfire Wars. Shane left the planet with an emergency departure ship. A special unit took refugees to several different planets whose local governments offered to take certain percentages of the refugees. Shane Aslat was taken to the planet Sheth. He went to several colleges there. The knowledge and wisdom that he received on Sheth was very helpful to him. From there, Shane moved to Bathannia's World where he lived above an intoxication joint. Drinking and gambling became part of his daily life. In one of his card games, he won a very fast fighter ship. Its previous owner was a bald warrior named Torra—a native to Bathannia's World. As soon as Shane saved enough credits from his gambling, he left Bathannia's World. He left the remote planet and hung with the Tyrris Militia space gang. The renegade pirates attacked other spaceships and stole riches from the innocent passengers. After several raids and assaults on unarmed ships, Shane left the Tyrris Militia. He went on his way, on with his life. Shane liked traveling through space, to other planets. He did not really know what he wanted in life.

The Telfire Wars began in the year 15073. The series of wars erupted in the Telneth Star System when the people demanded that the system's space freight monopoly be broken up. The freight company knew that if competition was formed, they would lose millions of credits. The Galactic Government would also lose if the freight monopoly was broken up. Because of this, the Galactic Government kept procrastinating the support that it had promised to the system's people. Finally, the government announced to the people that it chose not to be involved in the dispute. Soon after the announcement, many freight companies were formed. The competition became very fierce. The original freight company began modifying their ships with laser weapons and torpedoes. After they assaulted two other freighters, the majority of the competition began modifying their *own* ships. Many space battles occurred between the freight companies. Insurance for the products being transported rose drastically. It was a great opportunity for the insurance agencies. And to no one's amazement, the Galactic Government was collecting big credits from those agencies. The people of the Telneth System were extremely angered. An organized boycott was formed on the planet Alnor. Soon, the other planets of the system joined the boycott. Many people started transporting their own freight in their personal ships. As this became more and more popular, the space freight companies began firing on the civilian ships. Hundreds of innocent people were purposely killed. It was not until the public avoided the freight companies that the grudges came. It seemed that everyone wanted revenge. Many wanted to avenge their lost ones who had been killed. The war only escalated. One of the larger space freight companies mysteriously came across several massive nuclear weapons. A plan was devised by that company to systematically destroy each planet in the system. It did not take long for the classified information to reach the public; there were many disloyal people in the freight business. People were helpless against the companies. A plea was given to the Galactic Government asking for their help. Avoiding the Telfire Wars, the government repeated their position. They did not even want to help evacuate the people and save them from nuclear destruction. A fleet of ships from another system offered to evacuate the children. There was not enough room aboard for the parents; however, some of the more wealthy people managed to hitch a ride. Shortly after the evacuation, Alnor, Elbi, Bartu, and Shallum Ibner were destroyed. Millions of people died because the Galactic Government considered large amounts of credit more important than life.

Shane awoke to find someone coming into the hotel room. It was a woman. She had dark brown hair and blue eyes. She was very beautiful. She wore a short skirt that had been ripped. Fishnet stockings covered her long legs. Her blouse was half unbuttoned. She was surprised to see someone in her room.

"Who are you?" she asked.

"My name is Shane Aslat. Who are you?"

"I am Ariel Tion. Why are you in my room?"

"I didn't know it was your room. This is an old abandoned hotel. How was I supposed to know?"

"I guess you wouldn't know. By the way, you have a big, black spider crawling on your head."

Shane quickly sat up on the bed and flung it to the floor. His boot came crashing down on it. "It must have been another one from that barrel," he said.

"What barrel?"

"The one underneath the stairs on the first floor."

"What were you doing in a barrel?"

Shane looked at Ariel. She looked like someone he could trust. After a pause, he continued. "I was hiding from Galactic Government Troops. I'm on the run."

"Why are they chasing you? Did you look at 'em the wrong way?" Ariel asked wryly.

"Actually, I have some information they want."

Ariel shut the door and sat down in the chair. "What kind of information?"

"I have information on a treasure that they're looking for," Shane said.

"A treasure?"

"I don't know what kind of treasure. But they seem to want the information pretty badly. I was on the planet Selnaan when I came across the information. The government officials found out that I had it. I quickly started my ship and left the planet. Not too far from the planet, Galactic Government ships started chasing me. Laser fire was all around my ship. I sped up to lightspeed-plus, but I couldn't shake 'em. Finally, they hit my engines. The next thing I knew, I was caught in Yaraden's gravitational pull. My ship came crashing down outside of Metrocity. I was lucky enough to make it out of the ship with just a few bruises and a cut-up leg. The government officials landed and started chasing me on foot. The only safe place I could go was Metrocity. It started raining when I was cutting through the old factories and industrial areas. Then they chased me down the alley. And here I am."

"Yeah, they can be such a pain in the ass at times."

"So, why do you live in an abandoned hotel room?"

"I…am a harlot," she said. "And this is the only place I have to live."

"But the Galactic Government doesn't use currency. Surely, you don't have a computer account in the digital currency system for the work *you* do?"

"No, I don't. They would throw me in prison, if they found out I'm a harlot. I just trade my services for other services. It's not a very good life, but I survive. I'm stuck on this planet with no way off. I remember when I was young, Metrocity wasn't like it is today. Everything seems like it's changed," she said, her eyes staring into the distance. "My parents and I used to go on vacations once a year. We would go to other planets and see beautiful sites. The government killed them because they wouldn't join the new monetary system. I ran away, and the government couldn't find me. I've been living here ever since."

"You know, you don't have to be a harlot. You could get a job and better yourself," Shane said.

"I can't join the new system now, after it's already begun. The government would kill me for not joining when it first started. I'm just—"

"No. I mean outside of the Galactic Government's jurisdiction. There are plenty of jobs on the outside. And you have about ninety percent more freedom there too."

"How am I going to get there?" she asked.

"I'll take you there, if we can get to a ship without being noticed."

"You would do that for me? You don't even know me." She walked over and hugged him. "Thank you," she said. "You're the only man that ever said anything nice to me."

"Hey, it's no problem. I'm sorry for getting your bed wet with my clothes. It's pouring out there."

"Hey, it's no problem."

Shane smiled. He stood up from the bed. "I think we should stay here for the night. They already searched here. I don't think they'll be back. I can sleep in one of the other rooms," Shane said.

"No. I mean, that won't be necessary. There is plenty of room in here. Besides, all of the other rooms are very disgusting. I can sleep in the chair if you would like."

"Are you sure you wouldn't mind?"

"No, I wouldn't mind."

"You know, I think there is plenty of room in this bed for both of us. And I don't mean that in a sexual way. I just think it would be better if we both get some good sleep. We have a lot of work ahead of us tomorrow."

"All right. I'm not going to argue with that," she said.

They both made themselves comfortable in the bed.

"So, Shane, do you have someone special in your life?"

"Yeah, but I haven't seen her in quite some time."

"What's her name?"

"Shanda."

"I noticed your necklace with that name on it. How long has it been since you've seen her?"

"About a year."

"Wow. You should really go see her."

"Yeah, I plan on it."

They were both quiet for some time.

"Well, good night," she said, turning to the side of the bed.

"Good night."

Shane awoke from a dream. Cold sweat covered his face. He sat up on the bed. Ariel was still sleeping. Shane stood up and walked around the small room. He removed the historical document from his pocket. His eyes gazed at the ancient scroll.

Why is it that I get myself into these situations? Shane asked himself.

He sat down in the chair and put the scroll back into his pocket. Ariel stirred in the bed. Her eyes opened and she focused them on Shane.

"How long have you been up?" she asked.

"Oh, just a few minutes. I couldn't sleep. I had an awful dream."

"What was it about?"

"We were running from the government, but they knew our every move. It's like they were watching us from a tall tower overlooking the city."

"Huh. I wonder if that is supposed to mean anything."

"I don't know. But if I use my digital currency card, they will immediately know where I'm at. So, basically, I don't have any currency. That's not cool. Yeah, that's the only thing that I think the dream could have meant. If I use the card, they'll know where we're at," Shane said.

"How did they find out it was you who had the document?"

"They saw me carry the picture to my ship. From the markings on my ship, they found out my name."

Ariel started laughing. She stood from the bed and went into the bathroom.

"What's so funny?" Shane asked.

"What's so funny? I'll tell ya what's so funny. You are being chased over a treasure that might not even exist."

"That's true. But the guy that gave me the picture with the scroll inside it seemed to know what he was talking about."

Ariel came back out of the bathroom after cleaning herself up. She went to the closet and picked out some clothes for their upcoming trip.

"So, Shane, what does the scroll say?" Ariel asked.

"It says that it was written by the Scyllian Clan of Raatoris. It says that they discovered a majestic treasure in the Namaas Forest. It says that they built the Ojenis Temples in the forest to preserve it in. You know, Ariel, we studied about this in college. People—"

"You went to college?"

"Yes, I did. People have been trying to find this treasure for years. I can't believe that I actually have The Lost Scroll. This thing has quite a history in itself. I'm wondering why the government is so interested in this treasure all of the sudden."

"I don't know. Maybe they know what it is, but not where it is."

"That could be."

Shane stood up from the chair and went into the bathroom to clean up his sore leg.

"Do you have any bandages? My leg is cut up pretty badly."

"Yes. There are some in the top drawer."

"Okay, I got it."
After bandaging his leg, Shane came back out of the bathroom.
"So, are you ready to roll?" he asked.
"Ready as I'll ever be," she said.

Chapter Two

Straton Arnious was the leader of the Galactic Government from 15077 to the present time. He was a very cruel man. He was very determined to carry out the manifesto of the New Galactic Order. He was a man in his forties. Traces of gray were scattered throughout his black hair. He was one point seven meters tall.

The seat of the Galactic Government was on the planet Ishtorb. Straton sat at a large desk in a large office. A few green plants surrounded the room. Light came through a skylight window high above his desk. He leaned back in his comfortable chair and sighed. Just as he relaxed in his chair, the intercom sounded.

"Sir, yesterday, one of our undercover agents discovered a prostitute on the planet Yaraden," Straton's secretary said.

"What is her identification number?" Straton asked.

"Well, she doesn't have one."

"Are you telling me that she's not in the computer?"

"That's right."

"She never received an account number or a digital currency card. We'll fix that."

"Also, Shane Aslat was last seen in the same area."

"Ah, Shane Aslat. He thinks he is pretty clever, getting away with that document. What is his identification number?"

"Ah, let's see here. It is 6223416187746."

"Okay. I'll flag his account. If he uses his card, we'll find him. And about the prostitute…have the agent go back today and find her. I want her executed. No…have her thrown into prison with the men. That will be all," Straton said, turning off his intercom.

He looked at his computer screen and punched a few keys on the computer keyboard. A list of constitutional laws and regulations came onto the screen. The Galactic Government had so many laws, rules, and regulations, it was impossible for them to be printed into a single book. The entire collection of laws was kept in the Galactic Government's computer system. Very few disk libraries of the laws were in existence. Straton looked up several prostitute laws and reviewed them. He turned off the computer, a smile covering his face. At that moment, the door sounded.

"You may enter."

The door swiftly slid aside to reveal a tall, bald man. He stepped into Straton's office.

"So, Piross, I heard you discovered a prostitute on Yaraden. I was just talking to my secretary about the matter."

"Yes, she informed me to go back and arrest the harlot."

"She's not even in the computer system. I want her thrown into prison with the men. Go back and get her," Straton said.

"Yes, sir."

"Is there anything else that you need to talk to me about?"

"Yes, there is. It concerns Shane Aslat. He was last seen in Metrocity on Yaraden. We are searching the city with all of the resources that we have on that planet."

"I want him found, Piross. We need that document back. That document leads to something. There are a lot of Universal Expansionists interested in that document. The document is stirring up religion. It should be destroyed. I want all religion destroyed. Every Universal Expansionist will soon be in our control. We will expand beyond our present jurisdiction. We will control the entire galaxy. They cannot stop us. We are too powerful."

"They seem to have a losing battle on their hands."

"Yes, they do. If there is nothing more you need, then you may be dismissed."

"Yes, sir," Piross said, leaving the office.

Straton stood from his office chair and walked over to the window. He looked out into the greenery of his courtyard. The birds flew from tree to tree. There were a few butterflies roaming the grass. Straton stared into the trees.

I will crush the Universal Expansionists with all my might, he thought, a gleam of evil in his eyes.

In the year 4863 on Ancient Raatoris there existed a single mass of people. They were the Scyllian Clan. In the year 5181, the clan discovered a treasure on their planet. It must have been there for thousands of years. The treasure was discovered deep within the Namaas Forest. When the Scyllian Clan found this treasure, they were in a state of awe. They could not understand how the treasure initially got there. The Scyllian Clan built temples and colossal statues in the Namaas Forest where they had found the treasure. The Scyllian Clan mysteriously disappeared in 5612. They left behind evidence that they had discovered a treasure and built the Ojenis Temples to preserve it in. Everyone who searched, found it difficult to locate the Ojenis Temples in the Namaas Forest; the forest covered a third of the planet. The evidence that was left behind by the Scyllian Clan was in the form of a scroll. Other small pieces of evidence were also left behind by the clan, but through the years they had become scattered across the Tiffan Siram Galaxy. The scroll was later found by the Resofain Clan. There was a lapse of time between the disappearance of the Scyllian Clan and the formation of the other clans of Raatoris. The Resofain Clan's search for the treasure was to no avail. They had advisors come from off-world to consult them on the subject. They came to the conclusion that the Ojenis Temples did not exist. The scroll was then put into a Resofain museum where it was later stolen. The Stolen Scroll was found in the year 6946—one hundred and forty years after it had been stolen. It was found on another planet by Allio Naith. He was an engineer on the planet Onorra. The Stolen Scroll had been passed down through the generations of the Naith family. Then it became lost. The search for The Lost Scroll was minimal.

The later clans of Raatoris were scattered across various regions of the planet. They lived on mountains, islands, and in forests, swamps, deserts, grasslands, and tundra and ice lands. Each clan had many differences from the other clans. They saw the growing need for unity. There were too many disputes between them. A group of noble people came together from each clan and held the Raatoris Conference. The conference took place in 7108. At the meeting, the clans made many very important decisions. It was decided that since the Nesb Clan was the largest of the clans, their language—Nesbeoch—would be the official language of Raatoris. They agreed to form an empire to put an end to the Age of the Masses. The First Tiffan Siram Empire was formed in the year 7109.

When the Early First Tiffan Siram Empire—which was still occupied by the Notable Clans—started communicating with other local planets, they changed to a more usable language. The official language of the First Tiffan Siram Empire changed from Nesbeoch to Archineel. Archineel was used, prior to the change, in communications between most of the planets of the galaxy. Its origin was from the old, destroyed planet of Seelious. Seelious was destroyed when a drifting satellite collided into it. It was a most tragic occurrence.

The first emperor of the imperium was Saadi Duelthine from the Nesb Clan of Raatoris. He was responsible for seating the Imperial Throne of the First Tiffan Siram Empire on the planet Sulluth. The Notable Clans of Raatoris were the Nesb, the Amonis, the Rhen, and the Thesila. The other clans recognized them as such. The first seven emperors were from the Notable Clans. They were responsible for setting up the Early First Tiffan Siram Empire's foundation. After many houses ruled through the First and Second Tiffan Siram Empires, there was another period of interregnum. It started in the year 14995 and lasted for five years. During that period of time, a group of people came together to form the Third Tiffan Siram Empire. They decided that it would not go by that title. It was to be called the Galactic Government. It was not to be controlled by any one house. There were to be no emperors, empresses, presidents, regents, or protectorates, as there was in the past. There were to be leaders from a New Galactic Order. The Galactic Government was organized in the year 15000.

Through the centuries, the Tiffan Siram Empire had many different types of rulers. Some of them were very good rulers and others were tyrants. The recent formation of the Galactic Government (the Third

Tiffan Siram Empire) and its New Galactic Order had brought controversy throughout the galaxy. The Galactic Government of the Tiffan Siram Galaxy consisted of a vast number of planets that belonged to its federation. Not every planet in the galaxy was a member of the New Galactic Order, but quite a few were. Many of the planets in the galaxy were not as advanced as others. Most of them were different in society, economics, culture, religion, technology, and language. An elite group of ignorant people in the Galactic Government wanted to change all that. They wanted every last planet to be unified under the one government. There were those who did not want to join the New Galactic Order. The government wanted to bring everyone up to its so-called level of civilization. Their manifesto was slowly being carried out. More and more planets were joining their federation. Some of the planets were forced to join against their will. It had created a massive controversy.

Chapter Three

There were many different types of religions throughout the Tiffan Siram Galaxy. All creatures with a spirit needed religion. They all instinctively knew that there was someone greater than themselves. The primary religion in the Tiffan Siram Galaxy was administered by the Universal Expanse Church.

There was a great cause for religious unity during the Age of the Tyrants of the imperium. People usually wanted God's help the most when they were in trouble. That was primarily why the Kelv Wesnith Synod came to exist at that time in history. The people had no written word or law from God to live by. It had all been lost in history through the ages. Time washed it away. In the year 8217 the Kelv Wesnith Synod assembled together on the planet Troth to draft and create an acknowledgment of faith in the one true religion. The synod consisted of hundreds of different types of religions; however, they all had one thing in common: they knew that there was someone greater than themselves and they knew that it felt good inside when they loved others and were helpful to those in need.

In 8360 Adrex Stoughe composed the *Stoughe Creed.* The creed was a summary of the *Kelv Wesnith Synod Acknowledgment of Faith*. The creed consisted of five elements of canon law: the Creator made everything, the Creator has the power to perform anything that He wishes, He is in control of everything at all times, He is the All-seeing Eye, and His spiritual creatures should love Him and each other and be wise unto death. Adrex Stoughe died a martyr along with many other Universal Expansionists. He became a legend.

Archives were set up on Troth to contain and preserve the *Kelv Wesnith Synod Acknowledgment of Faith*, the *Stoughe Creed*, other ecumenical creeds, liturgical forms, and many other religious documents.

There were also religions in the galaxy that did not belong to the Kelv Wesnith Synod. According to the Universal Expanse Church, most of the other religions not belonging to them were cults full of evil people. In 9672, there was a religious crusade against many of the "evil" cults. The crusade destroyed a large portion of them, which hypocritically contradicted the fifth law of the *Stoughe Creed*.

Since the New Galactic Order came into existence, the Universal Expanse Church itself had dissipated by two-thirds. The Galactic Government's concept of religion was atheism. There were many heretics murdered by the Galactic Government.

Shanda Rubine was a beautiful woman who lived in the small, old-fashioned town of Almoss on the planet Myrath. Shanda was a Universal Expansionist in its generic sense. She loved the one true God, the Creator of all.

Shanda awoke from her sleep. She rubbed her eyes and looked out the window. The sun was shining. It was another beautiful day. She removed her blanket and sat up on the edge of the bed. As she yawned, she heard the birds singing their beautiful songs outside of her window. Shanda looked at her nude body in the mirror. Memories of Shane came back to her. It had been over a year since she saw him. She sat down in her bedroom chair and started to cry. She was very lonely. Her heart longed to see Shane.

She remembered when they first met. She was working in a restaurant attending a salad bar when Shane walked in. He had just left work and was very hungry. It had been a long day for him. He was an electronic technical engineer. He sat down in a booth and ordered a sandwich and salad. Shanda walked over to his table with his salad and their eyes met. Shane found Shanda to be very attractive. He asked her out. She knew they would hit it off pretty well.

Other memories flooded her mind as well. She remembered her best friend Troi who lived back on her home planet Pondu Norax VII. Shanda thought of the many things they used to do together. She longed to see her parents and her friend. She had not been on Pondu Norax VII for years.

"Oh, dear God, please let me see Shane again. I miss him so much. Please help me cope with my loneliness. Please give me strength to carry on. Amen," Shanda prayed.

She wiped the tears from her face and put on some clothes. After she was dressed, she went into the kitchen to see what she had to purchase from the market that day. She had a very small house. There were three rooms in the house: the bedroom, the bathroom, and the kitchen. She realized that she was running low on quite a few items. She did not have that much currency to purchase what she needed. The planet Myrath was located outside of the Galactic Government's jurisdiction. It was possible to use tangible currency there. Shanda walked into her bedroom and took the currency from a stand. As she put it into her pocket, she headed for the kitchen door. Outside, light gray clouds set out against the light green sky. The sun's light poked through the clouds occasionally.

"Good morning," one of her neighbors said.

"Hi. How are you?" Shanda asked.

"Oh, pretty good. How 'bout yourself?"

"Not too bad."

Shanda continued walking down the dirt street toward the market. The market was located at the end of the village, at the end of the main street. It was high noon, and most of the people were out doing the day's business. She walked past her place of employment and looked in the window. It was a wood furniture manufacturing company. She was a chair assembler. Most of the town's manufacturing businesses were closed a few days of each week. The town's market was open every day. Shanda noticed a commotion ahead of her. In front of the local intoxication joint, there were several men struggling. Someone's sword was drawn. It quickly came down through the air with the sun's light reflecting off its silver blade. A scream followed as a man fell to the dusty street. Shanda slowly walked past the intoxication joint, looking at the man on the ground. There was always someone dying at that place. Several men stared at her as she walked by, their evil eyes concentrating on her body. She glanced back and noticed them staring at her. Her pace quickened.

Most of the people that lingered about the intoxication joint worked for the evil Tulli whose dark castle overlooked the town of Almoss. Some of them belonged to a cult. The castle stood on a mountain, high above the town. Most of that region of Myrath was part of the Tulli Realm. Tulli usually did not bother the town's people.

The Tulli Realm was formed early in the colonization of Myrath. Its history began when Tulli conquered the small village of Almoss. He was a fierce warrior, but was only known and feared by the local people. Many other warriors joined his realm. Under Tulli's supervision, his warriors built him a castle on Mount Amor in his honor. Below the north side of the castle was the town of Almoss. The castle's position enabled Tulli to watch over "his" town. Below the south side of the castle was the Slave Sea. With a telescope, one could gaze across the sea as far away as Thisilia. Through the years Tulli became more aggressive. His warriors practically owned the intoxication joint in Almoss. As the town of Almoss grew, so did the Tulli Realm. Although the realm was growing, Emperor Tulli decided not to interfere with the town's businesses and merchants; he did not want to affect the local economy.

Shanda turned a corner and started walking down the main street. Several horses stirred up dust as they ran by. She saw the market at the end of the street. She noticed a lot of activity—more than usual. When she reached the market, she walked along the entrance, trying to make her way through the crowd. She stepped over to where the chickens were sold. Several cages sat on a long table. She saw a nice-sized chicken at the end of the table.

"I'll take that one at the end," Shanda said.

"This one?" the man behind the table asked, pointing to the cage at the end of the table.

"Yes."

"That will be five merits," the man said.

Shanda took the currency out of her pocket and gave it to the man.

"Thank you. Please come again."

Shanda picked up the cage and scanned through the crowd. There it was. She headed toward a table with bottled milk and fruit on it. She purchased a bottle of milk and a few lavender colored pieces of fruit. After leaving that table, she looked for some bread. Walking through the aisles, Shanda did not notice any bread or other grain products. Finally, at the last table, she discovered the bread.

"You are the only person with bread for sale today," Shanda said.

"Yes, I know. I guess no one felt like baking last night," the woman said.

"Yeah. How much is a loaf?"

"Three merits."

"Isn't that a little high?"

"Yes, but where else are you going to get it?"

"If you don't sell me a loaf for one merit, you can let it set and mold for all I care," Shanda said.

"Two merits," the woman said.

Shanda turned around and started to walk away.

"Okay, one merit."

Shanda shook her head and kept walking. She was heading back toward the street when, suddenly, an old woman grabbed the chicken cage in her hand. The old woman started running away with it.

"Hey, you thief, bring that back here!" Shanda yelled.

She ran after the old woman. It did not take long before Shanda caught up with her. Shanda grabbed the woman and threw her to the ground. The cage fell, startling the chicken. Shanda held the old woman on thc ground.

"What did you steal my chicken for?"

"Let me up. Let me up, now."

"Tell me why you took my chicken."

"I'm hungry, okay."

"And I'm not? That doesn't give you a right to take my food. Why don't you get a job and earn your food?"

"No one will hire me."

"They might if you clean yourself up a little."

"I've tr—"

"Get up," Shanda said, picking up her chicken cage. "Follow me."

The old woman stood up and looked at Shanda for a long moment.

"Just follow me."

She followed Shanda, who led her to the table where the chickens were being sold.

"I'll buy another one," Shanda said. "Here is five merits."

She took the currency out of her pocket and gave it to the man behind the table.

"Take a chicken of your choice," Shanda told the old woman.

The woman took a cage from the table. She looked at Shanda.

"Thank you."

"Don't thank me. Thank God, for He loves all of His creatures."

Shanda turned around and headed for home, a chicken cage in one hand and a bag in the other. As she passed the intoxication joint, she noticed that everything seemed to be the same. The dead man still lay on the ground in front of the entrance. Other men were still drinking whiskey and being violent. The men that were staring at Shanda earlier started following her. She sensed it. She turned around and saw them. They started chasing after her. The chicken cage and the bag that Shanda was carrying suddenly fell to the ground as she started running as fast as she could.

I can't run home. They'll find out where I live, Shanda thought.

She ran between two houses. The three men were right behind her. There was a clearing ahead. Shanda dashed through the clearing and into the woods. The footsteps were pounding behind her. She felt her heart beating rapidly. Dodging low branches and jumping over fallen trees, she quickly made her way through the woods. It was far beyond her understanding how she managed to leap over a wide stream. One of the men fell into the flowing water. The other two men kept chasing her. Shanda ran with all her might. The pain in her lungs was becoming severe. She gasped for air. The muscles in her legs were weakening. Her legs felt like they were going to collapse. She fell into the leaves below a large tree. Seconds later, the two men stopped at the tree. Shanda tried to slow her breathing. Sweat poured from her body. Her sweaty, blond hair was covered with dirt from the fall. The men picked her up.

"What do you want?" she asked, trembling.

"Emperor Tulli wants another beautiful female concubine for his chambers. You are now his. Do you understand?"

"I had a feeling you were from the Tulli Realm. Let go of me, now," Shanda yelled, yanking her arm from the grip of her captor.

The third man came to a stop where the others stood. His clothes were soaked. A smile covered his face.

"Thought you could get away, did you?"

They tied her arms with rope and led her on through the forest. They continued through the woods and on up the mountain toward the Tulli Castle. Shanda prayed for help as they led her to captivity.

Darkness filled the forest as night slowly settled. Shanda was extremely exhausted. Her captors continued to direct her up the twisted trails. She heard twigs snapping and the sound of leaves under her feet as she faded in and out of consciousness. She started experiencing previous events as they drifted through her mind. She saw the old woman that stole her chicken. She saw a sharp blade cut through the man at the intoxication joint. She saw Shane's ship lifting from the surface of Myrath. Then there was darkness. She opened her eyes. Her heart skipped a beat as she looked up and saw the tall, dark castle towering over them. She was led to an entrance in the rear of the dark castle. From there, Shanda saw the town lights of Almoss far below. The rigid cliffs frightened her further.

"Get in there," one of the men said, pointing to the castle entrance.

Her shirt became wet as she was slammed against the stone wall on the inside. Condensation covered the large, cold stones. It was almost a slime. They led her down a dark, narrow passage and up a few stairs. The air was extremely damp. The scent of mildew lingered in the passage. After a seemingly endless maze of passages and stairways, they stopped.

"I will go ask Norba if Emperor Tulli can be disturbed at this time. We must show him our presentation," one of the men said.

He left the room and disappeared around a corner. They stood in a circular room. There were three arched doorways in the room. One led to a corridor where the man had left. Another led to the stairway that they had just come up. The last one led to a wide stairway that led upward on a curve. The room had a cement floor and a red brick wall. Shanda noticed a window high above one of the arched doorways. A bat hung from its sill.

One of the two men followed Shanda's gaze high up toward the ceiling. "What's the problem, woman, never seen a castle before?"

Shanda looked at the man. "You're going to pay for this. All will be judged accordingly."

"All will be judged accordingly? What are you, one of those religious fools? What do they call them, Universal Expansionists? You think you can change the galaxy? You think wrong. You better think again. You're now just an intriguing piece of entertainment for Emperor Tulli's court."

"Ignorant fool," Shanda said, spitting on him.

He raised his hand and struck her across the face. She fell backwards to the cold floor, tears bursting from her eyes. The other man lifted her back to her feet.

"Don't you ever spit on me again."

Shanda looked down, tears dripping to the floor. A small puddle was starting to form at her feet. The man that had left returned to the circular room.

"Norba said that Tulli is in the throne room. Let's go," the man said.

They brought her up the wide stairway. It curved upward, like an endless spiral. Not far up the stairs, another stairway forked off to the right. The men turned and led Shanda up the other stairway. It also went upward on a curve. The stairs ended at a massive room. A fountain of flowing water was in the center of the room. Immense, marble pillars stood in each corner, their whitish-black color matching the squares of the floor. Directly across from them, Shanda saw large doors. Knights stood on either side of the doors. They wore blue tunics. Their matching blue pants were loosely fit around their boots. They both held long staves in their hands. Large, feathery helmets covered their faces. The three men brought Shanda across the floor toward the doors, their footsteps echoing throughout the room. They entered the throne room. Inside, Shanda surveyed the large statues on either side of the room. She saw a man at the other end. He sat on a large throne, a woman on either side, fanning him. Both women wore white dresses.

"Enter. Come, show me what you've brought."

They brought Shanda across the room to the foot of the throne. Tulli was an older man with wrinkled skin and gray hair; however, he was muscular. He wore a flowing white robe with black trim.

"Well, well…what a beautiful little thing. What's your name?"

Silence filled the room. The emperor's words were echoing through Shanda's mind.

"Shanda," she managed.

"Shanda," he repeated. "I want to welcome you to the Tulli Castle.

I think you'll find your stay here to be most enjoyable. Just think of it as a time of relaxation. You will be accommodated with all of the essentials. You will be here for quite some time, so get used to it. How did you get that bruise on your cheek?"

One of the three men stepped forward. "I hit her, Emperor Tulli. She spit on me."

"You've injured my prize. Now, you must die!" Tulli said.

He stood up and took a sword from the throne's side. The woman that was fanning him on that side stood back as he grabbed the sword. He pointed it straight at the man's face. His face went pale as he trembled in fear. Tulli lowered the tip of the sword to the man's throat and abruptly shoved it through until it slid out the other side. With a quick roll of the eyes, the man fell to the marble floor. Silence, once again, filled the room.

"Shanda, I apologize on his behalf. You two, bring her to my concubine chambers and have Norba come up here and take care of this mess."

"Yes, your majesty."

They led Shanda to a side door in the throne room. After taking the ropes off her wrists, they gestured her inside. Slowly, she entered the room. The door closed behind her. Several young, beautiful women lay on a large cushioned comforter. There were many fluffy pillows among the women. A thin, transparent curtain surrounded the room. In the rear of the room, there was a carpeted foyer. Shanda noticed a passage beyond the foyer. Most of the women wore negligées and other lingerie. Some of them were nude. As Shanda entered the room, a few of the women glanced up at her. She sat down on a small couch to the left of the large comforter.

"What's your name?" one of the other women asked.

"Shanda," she said with an expressionless face.

"You might as well make yourself comfortable, Shanda, it's going to be a long night."

Shanda met the other woman's gaze for a long moment and then closed her eyes. With a sigh, she lay down on the couch and stared at the ceiling.

An older woman entered the room from the rear passage. She walked over to Shanda. "Come with me. I must clean you up and prepare you for tonight."

• • •

A woman brought Shanda to Emperor Tulli's private chambers. The older woman was in charge of the concubines. She kept the women in line. As the older woman left, Shanda slowly walked into the large room. She looked around the entrance area. A closed chest sat in one corner. Across from a large wooden dresser sat a cushioned chair. The chair looked similar to Tulli's throne, except it was a much smaller version. Stepping farther into the room, she noticed an oval mirror hanging next to a cabinet. Gazing into the mirror, Shanda saw her beautiful body beneath the transparent negligée. Her flowing, blond hair slightly covered her breasts. The erotic gown revealed a hint of her vulva. She observed her firm ass and long thighs.

A quiver of fear overcame her as she thought of what was about to happen. Possibilities of escape crossed her mind. She knew the thought was too unrealistic. She continually tried to psychologically prepare herself for the sexual confrontation. With all her effort, she could not prepare for it. She knew that whatever was about to happen, it would leave an emotional wound. She kept imagining horrible thoughts. It did not seem to trouble the other women. Perhaps they were used to it. From what Shanda had seen, some of them seemed to enjoy it.

As she proceeded around a corner, she saw a wide bed with a canopy extending over it. Emperor Tulli lay propped up against the headboard. Two women were in the bed with him. One massaged his well-built body as the other performed fellatio. Like in the concubine chambers, the scent of sexual secretions filled the room. Shanda wanted to turn and run. She wanted to retain herself for Shane, the man she loved.

"Well, well… Shanda, what a surprise. I'd say you're a little overdressed for the occasion. Won't you slip out of your gown and come to me? You are looking quite desirable," Tulli said.

Chapter Four

Shane and Ariel walked along a railroad track. Yellow blades of grass stood up from between the railroad ties. Between the rails, old, white stones were covered with a black grease. Like most of the other tracks they had passed in the last few minutes, rust covered the rails. Trains had not run on the tracks for years. At one time, it had been a very active area. Most of Metrocity's distribution was done by truck now. Many buildings were on either side of the track. They were all old storage buildings.

"I sure hope there's a space freighter leaving Yaraden today. We don't need to be stuck here another night. The government troops are probably everywhere as it is," Shane said.

"I'm sure we can find a freighter. I see them coming and leaving all the time," Ariel said, her long, brown hair slightly blowing back from the wind.

"I just hope that we can hitch a ride without the government finding out. It's not gonna be easy."

"That's for sure."

Shane observed a few of the old buildings to his right. Most of them had large side doors located high above the ground. The doors had been used to load and unload the train cars. He could not help but notice a boxcar that—at one time—had derailed and impacted into one of the buildings. Apparently, no one ever cleaned up the mess. Perhaps it happened at the end of the railroad era and no one wanted to bother with it. Now, tall weeds and bushes grew around the boxcar. They continued to walk toward old downtown Metrocity.

"So, Shane, where were you raised?" Ariel asked.

"On the planet Elbi. The planet doesn't exist anymore. It was destroyed in the Telfire Wars. My parents were killed there. During the evacuation, my brother and I were separated."

"I'm sorry."

"Well, that's all in the past. The only thing that I have to look forward to now is my future…and that doesn't look very bright at the moment."

"I would tell you to cheer up, because everything will be all right. But, under the circumstances, I'll shut up."

Shane did not say anything. They just walked along the track. Ahead of them, the track set between two tall buildings. The buildings were very close to the track. The passage became narrow and shadowed from the sun. Shane looked up at the tall buildings. A few of the old, tan bricks had fallen from the very top of one of the two buildings. They lay on the ground next to the track, broken into many small pieces. His gaze then shifted from the bricks to the far end of the two buildings. Where the passage opened up on the other side of the two buildings, the shadows disappeared. Shane stopped in his tracks and stared at the far end of the two buildings.

"What's wrong?" Ariel asked.

"I have a bad feeling about this. At the end of the buildings down there—it looks like a good place for an ambush. I've had a feeling that we were being watched. I'm not gonna take any chances. Let's go a different way," Shane said, turning to the left.

She followed him at a fast pace. There was an alley ahead of them. As they entered the alley, they avoided stepping on trash that had been left there long ago. In the center of the alley, some of the old sewer drains were rotted through. Most of the surrounding buildings in the area were made from brick. Shane and Ariel were in the outskirts of old downtown Metrocity. Not very many people were around the old downtown. It had all been abandoned. The government did not want to reconstruct the old downtown. Instead, they built a new downtown. The new downtown could not be mistaken for the old; it had tall skyscrapers made from concrete, metal, and glass. Modern streets and walkways gave it a futuristic touch. There were many businesses around the new downtown Metrocity area. Ariel could just see the tip of one of the tall buildings through the trees in the distance. Could that be the tall building in Shane's dream? Perhaps they *were* being watched. Her gaze shifted from the tall building back to the buildings in the immediate vicinity. She scanned the nearby shadows. If there was anybody waiting there for them, she did not see them.

"Get down!" Shane shouted.

Ariel quickly fell to the ground next to Shane. Suddenly, a blue laser beam damaged a building wall next to them.

"Where did that shot come from?" Ariel asked.

"Over there, behind that small shed," Shane said. "I *thought* we were being watched."

"We have to start moving very quickly, if we're gonna make it out of here. There's a door over there. Let's get in that building now, before it's too late," Ariel said.

"You're right. Let's go."

Both of them headed for a door to their left. Another blast of laser fire just missed them as they entered the building.

"That was a close one," Ariel said.

"Too close."

Inside, the building was dark. There was just enough illumination for them to see where they were going. They ran toward a metal stairway that led upward.

"This way," Shane said. "Let's go to the roof. From outside, I noticed another building right next to this one. I think we can jump to the next roof."

"Okay," Ariel said, right behind him.

Shane leaped a few steps to the second level. They followed a narrow, metal catwalk that led across the old factory. The catwalk floor was made of metal grating. Soon, they found another stairway and climbed to the third level. Large metal pipes ran parallel to the floor. Wire harness ducts hung from the ceiling. Shane stopped at a door. There was a passageway perpendicular to the one they were on. He looked to the left and then to the right.

"Let's go to the right," he said.

They went through the door and turned right. The passage led them to a dead end.

"Oh, shit," Shane said.

"Wait. There's a ladder," Ariel said, pointing to a metal ladder to her right.

They climbed the ladder up a well that led through the higher levels. It ended at a warehouse on the fifth level. They stopped and looked at the large, empty warehouse. Thick dust covered the wooden floor.

"This must be the top level. Look, there's the ladder that leads to the roof," Shane said, pointing toward the side of the warehouse.

"I see it. Let's go," Ariel said.

They headed for the ladder. Halfway across the dusty floor, they heard a voice.

"Stop, right there."

They both turned around and saw a Galactic Government Trooper holding a laser rifle in his hands. It was pointed directly at them.

"I don't think you're going anywhere," the man said.

Shane and Ariel looked at each other.

"Let's go for the ladder, Ariel. They're gonna kill us when they capture us, so we might as well die running," Shane whispered.

"That's true," Ariel said.

"On three: One…Two…*Three!*"

They dashed for the ladder. The Galactic Government Trooper held up his laser rifle to the ladder. He fired. Light blue beams cut through the darkness of the warehouse. Ariel screamed as her leg was grazed. She managed to keep climbing. Shane pushed open the roof door. The man fired again. There was another scream from Ariel. This time, the beam scraped across her foot, just below her other wound. They leaped onto the roof, slamming the door behind them.

"Ariel, are you okay?"

"No. I can't stand the pain," she said, lying on the building's roof.

Shane quickly looked at the two wounds. They were not severe.

"Do you think you can make it to the next roof? It's about a meter across."

"I'll have to, I guess," she said, wincing from the pain. "I'm glad he doesn't aim well."

Shane helped her to her feet. Ariel ran with a terrible limp. Just as they jumped over the gap between the buildings, they heard the roof door open. The trooper popped his head out and saw Shane and Ariel on the next rooftop. He raised his laser rifle. There was a yell as he lost his footing and fell to the warehouse floor. They kept running. Shane noticed a line of old, connected boxcars far below. They extended across a bridge and through a few trees, disappearing from sight.

"We have to go down to the second level of this building."

"For what?"

"There is a line of boxcars down there. If we can get on them, we can leave this area."

"Let's go," she said.

They found the roof door to the building and made their way to the second level. There was a window one point five meters above the boxcars. Shane broke the glass with a nearby pipe. They jumped onto the top of the cars. Ariel shouted as her leg hit the top of the car.

"Are you all right?" Shane asked.

"Yeah," she said, tears rolling down her cheek.

Shane took her hand and they ran along the tops of the boxcars, jumping over the gaps.

After they crossed what seemed like a hundred boxcars, they came to a stop. They stood on the last car of the line. They were in an old residential neighborhood. A few houses were located on a small side street to their left. Several trees interfered with the view of the surrounding area.

"Let's see if we can get ourselves an anti-gravitational transport," Shane said, climbing down the metal ladder on the side of the boxcar.

"Yeah, we can't make it to the docking areas on foot without being noticed," Ariel said, following Shane down the ladder.

They stepped onto the rocky ground and headed toward the street to their left. Shane did not see any anti-gravitational transports parked on the street. As they walked down the street, they looked in the driveways next to the houses. There were no AGTs around.

"I don't think anyone lives around here," Shane said.

"I don't either."

"We'd better get out from the middle of the street. Let's walk along the front of the houses. We might have to quickly hide."

"You're right," Ariel said, moving toward the front of the houses.

When they reached the end of the street, they heard the hissing sounds of many AGTs traveling on a busy street nearby. The busy street could slightly be seen through a small patch of woods. Many AGTs and larger cargo AGTs traveled past the area. Shane took a glimpse around the backyard of one of the abandoned houses at the end of the street. He saw an AGT sitting there. A smile grew on his face.

"Come on, Ariel. I found one over here. You have to get off your feet. Your leg is bad enough as it is."

She followed him over to the AGT. Shane tried the door. It was unlocked. He opened it and rolled down the window. Walking around to the passenger's side, he opened the door for Ariel. She sat down. Her leg pounded and felt like a burning fire. The pain was revealed on her face.

"How are you going to start it?" she asked.

"I'll have to hot-wire it," he said.

Shane ripped at some wires underneath the dash. Ariel cleared her throat, trying to get his attention. He looked up at her. She held a set of keys in her hand.

"I *thought* I was sitting on something," she said.

Shane looked at Ariel. "Well, what do ya know?" He took the keys from Ariel's hand and started the AGT.

With a soft whine, the AGT rose from the ground.

"Let us go, shall we?" he said with a smile.

They backed out onto the street and headed toward a nearby corner. Soon, they turned another corner onto the busy street. The street led to the docking areas. Shane adjusted the rearview mirror. There was much traffic on the road. Several AGTs and cargo AGTs passed Shane as he gazed at the surrounding area. Many businesses were located on either side of the road.

"Make a right up here," Ariel said, pointing to a side street. "That way leads to the docking areas."

"Okay," Shane said, turning the corner.

They flew above an old, red brick street. Many industrial factories were located on either side of the street. Large semi truck cargo AGTs were parked along one of the buildings. The brick road curved to the left. Shane drove slowly, looking at the surrounding area. There was a stop sign ahead of them. The street ended at an alley.

"Which way?" Shane asked.

"Make a right."

After stopping at the sign, Shane turned right onto the alleyway.

More buildings surrounded them. Most of them were storage facilities.

"The sun's starting to go down. We better get to the docking areas fast," Shane said.

"It's not that far from here. Turn left at the next street."

"Okay."

Shane turned onto another red brick street. He scanned the surrounding buildings. They went straight for some distance. The sight of tall, mirrored-glass buildings caught Shane's attention. Light gray clouds covered the tips of the tall buildings.

"That's new downtown Metrocity," Ariel said.

"Yeah," Shane said. "Uh-oh."

"What?" Ariel asked as they came to a four-way stop.

"There is a road block ahead. It looks like Galactic Government Troops. Shit! What are we going to do?" Shane asked.

"I know a shortcut. Make a right between those two buildings up there."

Shane continued through the four-way intersection and turned right between two buildings. They entered a narrow alley. Discarded waste materials and other scraps of trash littered the alley.

"Those troops were staring right at us," Shane said.

"Yes, I know. We have to hurry."

"By the time—" Shane was cut short by the roaring engines of a shuttle that passed by overhead.

"Wow! We're closer than I thought," Ariel said.

"I guess," Shane said, stopping where the alley opened to reveal several shuttles and other spaceships.

The shuttle that had passed overhead was settling into one of the many docking areas. Shane turned left and drove toward the large spaceport.

"We're gonna have to play this cool," Shane said.

"I hear ya."

Shane drove to the rear of the large facility. The rear of the building was deserted. He stopped the AGT and turned it off. It settled to the ground.

"Let's roll," Shane said, opening the door.

Ariel followed him to the side of the building. They walked along the back of the building to where the loading area was located. Several trucks loaded boxes onto one of the transport shuttles. Shane noticed a supervisor standing near the loaders. They walked over to the man.

"Hi, there," Shane said.

"What can I do for you?" the man asked, surprised to see strangers in his loading area.

"Would you be kind enough to tell me where this shuttle is headed?" Shane asked.

"I don't see why not. This load is going to be shuttled to one of the space freighters waiting in the shipping lanes above Yaraden. We haven't had this many ships waiting in line out in the shipping lanes since the SR Series Robots were being manufactured. I think the name of the ship that this load is being shuttled to is called *Aarian's Freighter*. Some freelance captain named Aarian and his partner, Tross, have been coming to Yaraden for years. One of their other big stops is Obrah. This is the only shipment that Aarian is receiving this week, though," the man said.

"Oh, that's interesting," Shane said, remembering Tross's name from long ago.

"Yeah. Well, if you two don't mind, I have a lot of digital memory units to drain into the mainframe."

With that, the supervisor left and headed toward a door along the building. At that moment, the loaders were at some other part of the docking areas. It was the perfect opportunity. After the supervisor disappeared, Shane and Ariel ran for the open cargo bay. They dove into the dark cargo bay and hid behind a few of the boxes. Soon, the loaders came back and shut the shuttle's air-lock door.

"I wonder what this thing's hauling."

"Open one of the boxes," Ariel said.

Shane was tearing apart one of the boxes when he heard the shuttle's engines start up. He continued to open the box. To his surprise, he found a box of food inside.

"There's food in these boxes...I think. It is pretty dark in here," Shane said, examining the box in his hand. "Yes, it is food."

"That's cool. I'm starving," Ariel said.

"Yeah, me too."

The shuttle lifted from the surface of Yaraden, its anti-gravitational units switching on.

CHAPTER FIVE

A LONG TABLE sat in a large hall. The table was covered with an assortment of food. Several men and women sat around the table. One of the men was the leader of the Galactic Government. Straton Arnious sat in front of a large cooked turkey that had been flavored with many spices. There were many different types of meats along the table. Straton had a plate of food sitting in front of him. A tall glass of some exotic beverage sat close to his plate. A look of wonder covered Straton's face. His expression was noticed by the others. Straton had just seated himself minutes before the drink was served. He looked around the table and smiled.

"To whom do I owe the pleasure of this feast?" Straton asked in a voice that everyone present heard.

"It is I who made the arrangements for this dinner to be prepared in your honor," a large man said, walking into the room from a nearby entrance.

Straton looked up at the man. Silence fell over the table. To Straton, the silence was very loud. The man that stood in the doorway was someone that Straton had not seen for years.

"Boris Anathor. You've returned," Straton said, standing from his chair. "You said you'd never come back. You agreed that I won the game. Why have you returned?"

"Now, now, Straton, I agreed that you won the game of politics, but I never agreed that I wouldn't return. You must be mistaken about that part. I've seen the job you've done with the New Galactic Order since you've been in power. I think you've done an excellent job."

Boris walked over to the end of the long table and sat himself in one of the comfortable chairs.

"I've taken the liberty to invite your dignitaries and advisors to this special occasion. Quite the feast. Won't you sit and enjoy it, since it *is* in your honor."

Straton sat back down and stared at Boris. Boris started eating the food on his plate. After a few bites, he took a drink of his beverage. Straton managed to grip his fork and eat a bite of his food.

"Delicious, isn't it?" Boris smiled at Straton.

The other government officials around the table ate their food, trying to comprehend what the two men were discussing. Straton started getting nervous. Not one of his dignitaries had mentioned the dinner to him. Why the surprise? Why did those dignitaries of his let Boris persuade them into this lavish buffet? It had been years ago when Straton and Boris played the little game of politics. They gambled to see who would become the leader of the Galactic Government back in 15077. It was a high risk gamble. The loser was very unpopular for quite some time.

"You look rather uncomfortable, Straton. Has it been one of those days? Are you having troubles managing the government? Don't worry. Enjoy your dinner. Relax. We have so much to talk about," Boris said.

"So, what have you been doing for the last eleven years?" Straton asked.

"Oh, just hanging around the galaxy. I've been outside of the government's jurisdiction. It seems there are quite a few power-hungry emperors around the galaxy. There seems to be quite a few Universal Expansionists around too."

They quietly ate their food. The amount of food on the table was far more than enough to feed them all. Most of the dignitaries thought that Straton would be delighted to see Boris. From Straton's expression, they thought wrong. What was the conflict between the two men? It was a question that most of the dignitaries asked themselves.

"So, did you get any locations where the Universal Expansionists are?" Straton's secretary addressed Boris at the end of the table.

"Well, I—" Boris was cut short from Straton as he spoke.

"You never answered my question. Why have you returned?" Straton asked, rubbing his chest.

Boris looked at his watch. "I've come back to kill you, Straton…and all of your dignitaries. I've come back to reclaim what is mine."

Straton and his dignitaries started gasping for air as they fell to the floor. Some dishes fell to the floor, shattering.

"What have you done?" Straton screamed.

Seconds later, the room was silent. Boris stared at the only other person at the table.

"Nice work, Amminar. Great timing."

"Poisoning the food was not a problem, Boris. It will be much more difficult to straighten out this government than it was to kill its top officials."

"Yes, it will. Straton was not a very good leader. I'm sure that I will have this government expanded throughout the Tiffan Siram Galaxy much quicker. And I think we should disregard the name of the government. Galactic Government is not quite what I had in mind. Its proper name is the Third Tiffan Siram Empire. That is what it will be called from now on. I think we should start working on our master plan. The first part went well, don't you think, Amminar?"

"Yes, indeed. It sure did," Amminar said, gazing about the floor at the dead bodies.

They finished their dinner and left the room.

People expected the galactic economy to get better under the New Galactic Order. Unfortunately, it got worse. The Galactic Economics Exchange Council (GEEC) was an organization created by the House of Tymor during the era of the Second Tiffan Siram Empire. Emperor Semadian Tymor established the organization in 14831.

For those planets that belonged to the New Galactic Order, buying power was weakened when the federation was established. According to the so-called expert economists, the galactic economy was supposed to get better when the New Galactic Order was organized. However, the new system enabled the wealthy to become more wealthy and the indigent to become more indigent. The new system did not seem to be working very well (with the exception of the wealthy).

Credit limiting was at an all time low under the New Galactic Order. With some exceptions, anyone who tried could get credit. The New Galactic Order wanted it that way so more and more people would go into debt. The more people that were in debt, the more control the Galactic Government had on those people's lives.

The monetary unit of the New Galactic Order was an intangible credit in a computer system. Everyone in the Galactic Government's jurisdiction had to have a number assigned to them. It was their account number in the computer system. They had access to their credits from a government-issued digital currency card. The hours people worked at their place of employment were converted to credits and transferred directly into their accounts. When the people purchased products or services, the amount was deducted from their account via their digital currency card. With this system the New Galactic Order had the potential to know virtually everyone's whereabouts. They could also know everything that everyone owned. The only thing good about it was that it lowered the galactic crime rate.

The Galactic Government put people in prison and executed many people for committing so-called crimes. Most of the laws concerning the crimes were enforced to have more control over the people. Most of the laws were not even practical. The laws brought forth no sign of human rights. In fact, the laws took human rights away.

Those planets that were not part of the New Galactic Order did not have a buying power problem. Buying power was moderate for most of the people on those planets. They had many credit limits when it came to purchasing. But they had more trust in their fellow man when it came to loans. Sometimes people did not have to give any collateral when they borrowed. They had more trust in each other. Financial institutions stressed to the people the point of saving merits. According to the institutions, people would appreciate things more. The planets not federated with the New Galactic Order used the old currency which was used under the First and Second Tiffan Siram Empires of the Tiffan Siram Galaxy. The currency was called the merit. The merit was divided into ten sub-merits. Given the choice between the economic system of the New Galactic Order—which was regulated by the Galactic Economics Exchange Council—or the economic system of the planets outside of the Galactic Government's jurisdiction, most people—excluding Galactic Government officials—would prefer the merit currency system.

The news media of the Tiffan Siram Galaxy was controlled by the Galactic Government. What the government wanted the people to hear is what they heard. The news media within the Galactic Government's jurisdiction was known for providing false information to the people. It was a government stratagem to give them power over people who were the anti-government type.

There was no monopoly on the news scene in the Galactic Government, but there were only a few well-known agencies. There existed a vast network of telecommunication system satellites throughout the Galactic Government. They were used for government purposes, monetary purposes, news media, business, commercial, and private communications. Most of the communications were monitored by the government. The news media outside of the Galactic Government's jurisdiction was minimal and slow. There was no well-known agency.

Chapter Six

Aarian sat at the controls of his space freighter, gazing at the darkness of space. He noticed the other liners and freight ships as his ship drifted out from the shipping lanes of Yaraden. The ship's bridge was dark. There was no illumination with the exception of light from the distant stars. The starlight came through the observation window in front of Aarian. His attention went from the observation window back to an old space map. He, once again, surveyed the map.

"It's near impossible to read this map in the dark. Tross, can you see how long it will be before the technicians have the lights working again?" Aarian said to the only other person on the bridge.

"Sure. Where did you find that old space map, anyway?" Tross asked.

"In the bridge closet over there. This thing's very interesting. But I'm sure pleased to have a computer in place of these old maps. I remember when my old partner, Adarr, and I were using one of these maps. Man—I tell you—those are memories from the past. I kind of have to dust the cobwebs from my brain. It's been a long time. We got lost navigating with one of these maps once. We ended up in some weird star system. Luckily, we found our way back on course. I'd definitely rather have the computer coordinated systems."

"Yeah, I hear ya," Tross said, contacting one of the ship's technicians on the intercom. "It will be a couple of hours yet before we have light."

"Okay," Aarian said, folding up his map. "Did you have someone unload the shuttle yet?"

"The shuttle's bay is open, but they're not going to unload it until we have lights," Tross said.

"Yeah, I guess it would help if they had some light. I'm tired. It's been a long day. I'll be in my quarters, if you need me."

"Okay."

Aarian left the bridge as the door swiftly slid aside with a hiss.

Shane and Ariel crouched in a corner of the dark docking bay. Behind them, a large, metal beam stretched from the floor to the high ceiling. Where the beam met the ceiling, it connected to one of the many other structural beams. Their eyes were fixed on the crew members attending to their tasks. They had just left the shuttle's cargo bay moments before. The large shuttle sat in the center of the docking bay. Its hull had a bluish-purple tint to it because of the darkness in the bay.

"So, what's your plan?" Ariel asked.

"We have to find a place to hide so I can think of one."

Shane peered along the wall next to them. Toward the other end of the docking bay, he saw a metal grille in the wall.

"Over there," Shane said, pointing toward the other end of the wall. "There's a ventilation duct. Let's go."

They made their way along the docking bay wall. When they reached the ventilation duct, Shane pulled at the grille. It would not budge.

"I don't know why the lights are off, but if they come on now, someone's going to see us," Shane said. "And this thing isn't moving."

"Try pushing inward instead," Ariel suggested.

Shane pushed the metal grille. It opened, moving to one side on hinges. They smiled at each other. As they crawled through the dark duct, they heard the distant roar of the ship's massive engines. Shane thought he felt something fall out of his pocket, but he paid no attention to it. After a few ninety-degree turns to the left and right, Ariel said something.

"What is it?" Shane asked, looking at the darkness behind him.

"Oh, I just bumped my sore leg against a stupid piece of metal."

"Are you okay?"

"Yeah. I think so," she said.

They continued along the ducts until they came to an illuminated area. It was a widened area, but the height remained the same. The light came through a grate at the top of the duct. They stopped directly below the grate. Shane looked up through the grate and saw the metal beams of the docking bay ceiling high above.

"I think we're directly below the docking bay. We—" Shane stopped talking as the lights went out, flickered, and then came back on.

"They must be trying to restore the ship's lights," Ariel said.

"Yeah, I think they just fixed them. Let's move back away from the grate, just in case someone looks down here."

They moved toward the wider end of the duct where there was less illumination. Leaning their backs against the duct wall, they sighed.

"Now, maybe I can do some thinking," Shane said as he looked at Ariel.

"Yeah," she said.

Shane noticed her beautiful figure. Something suddenly came over him. He could not help but notice her breasts as she leaned over. He abruptly became erect. She noticed his eyes. He turned away quickly. There was a time when he would have had sex with anyone, but that time had passed. Suddenly, his thoughts were flooded with Shanda. He remembered when they were together. He remembered pleasing her. He remembered all the beautiful times they spent together. He loved her so much. He could see her sad face as his ship lifted from Myrath.

I have to see Shanda. I have to. Oh, how I miss her, he thought. He felt his sexual urge. *Control yourself, Shane. Control...*

Ariel tried to close her shirt a little more. "I'm sorry, Shane. I didn't mean to expose myself to you like that. I don't know what you're thinking, but I didn't enjoy being a harlot. And I don't want to be one anymore. I'm looking forward to getting out of the Galactic Government's jurisdiction so I can start a new life. I want to get a real job. I want to have a real relationship with someone. And I know we're not out of the woods yet, but I want to thank you again for helping me. You're a good friend."

"You're welcome," Shane said.

They both gazed up at the grate in front of them as a few crewmen walked across it.

"I think we should try to make our way to the bridge and plead with the captain to take us out of the Galactic Government's jurisdiction."

"Are you crazy? He might turn us over to the government," Ariel said.

"Do you remember when that supervisor at the spaceport told us the captain and his partner's name?"

"Yeah."

"Well, it just happens that I know Tross. We used to hang in the same intoxication joint. He owes me a favor," Shane said.

"Oh, really?"

"Yes. I think Aarian and Tross can be trusted, but I don't know about his crewmen. That's why I think we should continue on through these ducts. Hopefully, we can find our way to the bridge."

The sound of the ship's engines soon faded as they continued crawling through the ventilation ducts.

Aarian suddenly awoke from the sound of his intercom. He sat up on his bed and rubbed his eyes.

"Yeah?" he asked.

"Aarian, we now have lights throughout the entire ship. Do you want me to have them unload the shuttle now?" Tross asked.

"Ah, I'll oversee the operation. I haven't been down to the docking bay in quite some time. All right?"

"All right," Tross said, turning off the intercom.

After sipping on some beverage that sat on a table next to the bed, he stood up and left his quarters. The ship's corridors had very shiny floors. Fiber optic illuminators were spaced evenly along the walls. Aarian came to a corridor intersection and made a left turn. At the end of the corridor, there was an elevator. He rode the elevator down a couple of levels. When the door slid aside, he stepped out onto the upper level of the docking bay. The upper level consisted of a large, metal platform that overlooked the entire docking bay. To his right, there was a control room behind the large platform. Aarian saw a few crew members through the control room window. They were accomplishing various tasks. To his left, a stairway connected from the platform to the docking bay below. The entire platform and accompanying stairway were painted with yellow and black stripes. He made his way down the metal stairs to the lower level of the docking bay. Below, he saw the shuttle fixed in the center of the floor. There were two large loaders lifting the shuttle's cargo from its bay. Other loaders and heavy equipment were stored underneath the upper level section of the docking bay. There were several areas for storage along the docking bay walls. Aarian reached the bottom of the steps and headed toward the shuttle. He noticed the shuttle's pilot standing next to the front of it.

"How ya doin'?" the pilot asked.

"All right. How are you?"

"Not bad. I thought you'd never get the lights working."

"Yeah, I know. My partner just informed me that they were on. So, I thought I'd come down here and oversee the unloading of the shuttle. I've been in the freight business for fifty-one years. I've gone through two partners before Tross. And do you know how many times I've overseen the unloading of cargo shuttles?"

"How many?" the pilot asked.

"This is about the fifth time. I think my crew members handle themselves pretty well," Aarian said. His pride in his employees could be seen in his expression.

"They look like they're doing a great job to me," the pilot said.

"I'm sorry, my name is Aarian—which you probably already know. And what is yours?"

"Terrsil. Glad to meet you."

"Well, Terrsil, did the spaceport on Yaraden tell you that we'd be back in a week?" Aarian asked.

"Yes. I told them that it was not possible for you to unload the shuttle in the dark. They knew you had to be on your way to your next stop. Tross contacted me from the bridge and told me the lights were going to be repaired on your way to your next stop. I told the spaceport the situation and they understood. They have enough shuttles to manage for a week. So, where will I be staying for the week?"

"Tross had some quarters established for you on the fourth level. I'll have him come down and show you them as soon as this is unloaded," Aarian said.

"That would be fine. So, where is your next destination?"

"Obrah. It sets on the Galactic Government's border," Aarian said.

Their attention was drawn to the cargo bay. The loaders lifted skids of boxes and crates. They sat the skids along a wall of the docking bay. As soon as the cargo bay was empty, Terrsil shut the door.

"I'll move the shuttle to make room for the next shuttle at Obrah. Where do you want me to move it?" the pilot asked.

"I think if you move it over there to the left, we'll be able to fit another shuttle in here," Aarian said, pointing to the side of the docking bay.

"Okay, I'll do that," the pilot said, walking toward the shuttle entrance.

Aarian stepped out of the way as the shuttle slowly rolled across the docking bay floor. As Terrsil moved the shuttle, a crew member walked up to Aarian.

"I noticed you were down here. I have a question. One of the boxes on a skid was open. How should I handle this for inventory purposes?" the woman asked.

"Let me take a look."

They walked toward the storage area next to the docking bay wall. She showed him the skid with the open box on it. Inside the box, several smaller boxes of food were missing.

"Just call it a full box. It was probably some spaceport employees on Yaraden," Aarian said.

"Okay. Thanks," the crew member said, punching several buttons on a digital memory unit. She walked toward the yellow and black stairway.

As Aarian turned his attention toward the shuttle, his eyes came across something. He turned back toward the ventilation duct. The grille was open. He walked over to the duct entrance and shut the grille. He noticed something else. Inside, there was a book. He opened the grille back up and picked up the book. It was a book of poems. After closing the grille, once again, he walked back toward the shuttle. Terrsil was waiting for him.

"I'll send Tross down in just a few minutes."

"Okay."

Aarian made his way to the bridge with the book in his hand.

• • •

The metal ladder was cold. Shane and Ariel felt the frigid air as they climbed upward. A white frost covered the duct walls. A steamy mist came from their mouths when they exhaled.

"Shit, is it ever cold. I'm freezing. I wonder what section of the ship we're in," Ariel said.

"This is probably where the cooling systems are located," Shane said.

They continued climbing the ladder until it ended at a small room. After climbing out of the ladder well, they looked around the small room. A door was straight ahead of them.

"It's warmer up here," Ariel said.

"That's for sure. I wonder where we are," Shane said, looking at the door.

"There's only one way to find out. I'm ready when you are," Ariel said.

They walked toward the door. As they approached it, the door slid open to reveal…

"Oh, this is cool!" Shane gazed at the vast array of computer equipment.

Many displays, meters, and flashing lights surrounded the room. A holographic transducer was located in the center of the room. There were two other doors in the room—one to their left and one to their right.

"What are you so excited about?" Ariel asked.

"There is a holo-generator," Shane said, pointing to the center of the room. "We can recall a layout of the ship. We'll find the bridge in no time."

"Oh."

Shane walked over to a keyboard and punched a few keys. He looked at a display and punched a few more keys. Seconds later a holographic image of the ship's layout was displayed.

"How did you know how to do that?" Ariel asked.

"All holo-generators use the same system. Let's see here." He looked at the holographic image. "We're right here," he said, pointing. "And the bridge is…right here. It looks like we have to go out the door to our right, down a corridor to the left, and up an elevator to the next level. Then we have to go down another corridor to the right, make another right, and we should be on the bridge."

"Can you remember all that?"

"Yeah, I think so," Shane said, switching off the display.

They headed for the door. When it opened, Shane peered down the corridor in either direction. It was clear. They went out the door and turned left. It was very quiet. Shane tried to prevent his boots from echoing throughout the corridor. After they were inside the elevator and the door shut behind them, Ariel started laughing.

"There's that laugh again. Now what's so funny?" Shane asked.

"You, trying not to make any noise with those boots. If only I had a camera…"

"Ha, ha," Shane said, pushing the elevator controls.

Soon, the elevator stopped and the door opened. A crewman stood in front of them.

"How ya doin'?" Shane asked as he put his arm around Ariel and forced her to walk out of the elevator with him.

"Pretty good. How 'bout you two?"

"Great," Shane said.

The man entered the elevator and the door shut behind him. Shane and Ariel looked at each other.

"Were you going to stay in there?" Shane asked as they turned right.

"Sorry. I didn't know what to do. You're pretty smooth. You know that?"

"Hell yeah, I am!"

"Give me a break."

They walked toward a corridor intersection and made a right. A door stood in front of them.

"This should be the bridge," Shane said.

He took a deep breath and they entered.

A man with gray hair sat at the controls of the ship. Through the reflection in the observation window, Aarian saw them enter the room. He swiveled around in his chair.

"Hi. You must be Aarian," Shane managed after a few seconds of silence.

"Yes, I am. And you must be the person who opened a box of food in our shipment on the shuttle," Aarian said.

"Well, we *were* a bit hungry," Shane said.

"So, what do you want? Why did you stow away on the shuttle and come here?"

"Well, first of all, I want you to know that I'm an old friend of Tross. Second, we need a ride to the other side of the Galactic Government's jurisdiction. Tross owes me a favor," Shane explained.

"That's very interesting. In trouble with the government? From the few military powers in this galaxy, you had to pick the wrong one to mess with, didn't you?" Aarian said.

"Well, I—"

"Well, nothing. I don't want to know why they're after you. Don't tell me. Tross is my business partner, and I respect his debts. If he owes you a favor, then I'll help you. I'll take you as far as the border, but that's it. That's the direction we're heading in anyway. Our destination is Obrah. *I* sure don't need to be chased by the government. I think this belongs to you," Aarian said, holding up a book.

"My book of poems. Where did you—"

"At the entrance to the ventilation duct."

"Ah, I see. By the way, my name is Shane Aslat and this is Ariel Tion," he said as he received the book.

"Nice to meet you," Aarian said, looking at Ariel.

"Nice to meet you too," she said.

The bridge door opened. Everyone's attention turned to the door.

"I accommodated the shuttle pilot with—" He stopped talking and looked at Shane. "Shane! Shane! What a surprise. What are you doing here?" Tross asked.

"Remember that favor you owe me?"

"Yeah."

Tross remembered back when Shane saved his life. They had been sitting on the stools at the counter, drinking. They must have been there half the night when Tross began shouting and making a fool of himself. He insulted a Tarofain sitting at a table nearby. The alien stood up from his chair. He was three meters tall! He drew a laser pistol from its holster. The alien was going to kill Tross. It took Shane three hours to convince the Tarofain that Tross was not worth killing.

"Well, I need it. The Galactic Government's after me. I have to leave its territory," Shane said.

Tross continued to stare at Shane, startled to see him there.

"I've agreed to take them there. We'll have to think of some way to get them down to Obrah. I don't think they'll suspect anything. There aren't many government troops or officials on Obrah anyway," Aarian said.

"What have you been doing with yourself?" Tross asked.

"Well, after I left Bathannia's World, I became a member of the Tyrris Militia. Then I found a job as an electronic technical engineer. Now, I'm on the run," Shane said.

"Wow. Yeah, we sure did have some wild times in that intoxication joint back on Bathannia's World. Remember the time you won that ship from that dude. Huh, that was a good game," Tross said, a smile covering his face.

"Yeah, I see your hair's still long too. What have you been doing with *your*self?" Shane asked.

"After I left Bathannia's World, I found a job with Aarian here. His other partner, Adarr, died."

"So, you're an electronic technical engineer?" Aarian asked.

"Well, I used to be until about a week ago. Now, I'm a professional journeyman." Shane smiled.

"The reason I asked was because our lights have been going out lately. Our artificial gravitation almost went last month. Everything on the ship that was very light and not fastened down started floating away. We had to fix that quickly, I'll tell you. When it was repaired, everything stopped drifting and fell to the floor. It was a mess," Aarian said.

"I can troubleshoot the light problem if it happens again," Shane offered.

"Thanks. That would be appreciated. The technicians may have repaired it the right way this time, though," Aarian said.

"I can prepare you two quarters to stay in during our trip. Do you two want separate quarters?" Tross asked.

"Yes, that would be fine," Shane said.

"You haven't introduced me to this fine looking lady yet," Tross said.

"This is a friend of mine, Ariel Tion."

"Glad to meet you, Ariel," Tross said.

"Thank you. And I'm happy to meet you," Ariel said.

"Well, I'll show you two to your quarters, then," Tross said.

"She needs to attend to her wounds. And can we get something to eat?"

A man walked along a walkway. Troth's sun was shining bright. It gave the surrounding trees an array of brilliance. He walked toward a massive structure. It was an immense building with pillars of stone on either side of the entrance. The man wore a white robe with a rope tied around his waist. The temple before him was the original and the main Universal Expanse Church. He reached the bottom of the steps that led up toward the towering pillars. He had received a message that the minister wanted to see him. As he reached the arched doorway, he noticed several young boys and girls attending to special tasks. They were preparing for that night's service. Some children gathered ancient relics. Others prepared small green plants for the service. The man walked past the children and continued down the corridor. The corridor was very wide and long. High above, the ceiling arched to a point. Several doors were spaced evenly on either side of the corridor. Along the walls, there were pictures of intriguing characters. The man's robe fluttered as he walked beneath a large ceiling fan. Soon, he stopped at a door to his right and knocked.

"Come in." He heard the remote voice.

He entered the room. An old rug covered a hardwood floor. Many shelves were filled with books. A man sat at a desk across the room.

"You wanted to see me?" the man in the white robe asked.

"Yes, Leenith, I did. Have a seat. Make yourself comfortable," the man behind the desk said.

Leenith placed himself in an old leather chair in front of the desk.

"You've been my assistant minister for quite some time now. As a minister's aide, you have helped me make many decisions in the past. I need you to advise me on a new situation that has arisen. The Universal Expanse Church has been through a lot. Many heretics have been murdered by the Galactic Government. We've seen martyrs die for God throughout the Tiffan Siram Galaxy. We are a remnant of what there once was. There are many Universal Expansionists, but nowhere near what there once was. Leenith, something is about to happen. The Galactic Government has faltered. A new leader has taken over. His name is Boris Anathor. He is now calling it the Third Tiffan Siram Empire. Leenith, he has sent me a communique. He wants the Universal Expanse Church to unite with the government to become a team—if you will. What do you think our stand should be on this? They have been murdering our people for years. Now, a new guy comes along and wants to change everything. I think that if the new leader is serious about this, there are many new things that could come out of this merge. We could make laws that would encourage people to come to church. I think God would be pleased to have the galaxy's people under his church. What do you think?"

Leenith did not say a word. He just sat there staring at the minister.

"Are you all right?"

"Yes. I just don't understand why and how this has happened all of the sudden. Who is this new guy? Why is he interested in the church so much?"

"Perhaps his intentions are good. Just think, we—the Universal Expanse Church—could take part in making the laws of the galaxy. Wouldn't things be much better for people? In turn, the government officials and all of the galaxy's people could take part in the church. I think it would make them better people."

"Well, Thorton, that sounds relatively good, but there are a couple of questions."

"What?"

"What if all the other governments on the outside of the Galactic Govern—Third Tiffan Siram Empire's—territory do not want to join with us? Also, there are some church organizations on the outside here—besides us—that are not cults. They just don't share the same name or the same practices as we do. But they still love God. And the second question is: What if this Boris Anathor is lying?" Leenith said.

"Well, I personally don't think he is lying. But there is only one way to find out. And if the rest of the churches and people here outside the Third Tiffan Siram Empire's jurisdiction don't want to unite with the rest of the galaxy, well, there are ways to persuade them. I don't think a few people should obstruct the pleasure of God. I think it would displease Him," Thorton said.

"Well, perhaps at this point the other churches are not the issue. I agree that the only way to find out if Boris is lying is to call his bluff."

"You're right, Leenith," Thorton said. After a pause, he continued. "I'll send Boris a communique right away."

Chapter Seven

A shuttle settled in the docking bay of *Aarian's Freighter* with a slow, smooth motion. It sat across from the other shuttle in the docking bay. Several crew members were appointed to load the shuttle. The many skids of food were loaded onto the shuttle to be brought down to Obrah. One of the crew members came down the stairs toward the shuttle that had just arrived.

"Hi, there," the crew member said to the pilot.

"Hi," the pilot said.

"Aarian would like to talk to you about something."

"Oh, okay."

"Can you find your way to the bridge?" the crew member asked.

"Yeah, I've been up there a few times when I came to pick up shipments in the past."

"Okay," the crew member said, turning his attention to the loading of the shuttle.

The pilot headed for the bridge.

• • •

Upon reaching the bridge, the pilot was welcomed by Aarian.

"How are you doing, Aarian?" the pilot asked, shaking the captain's hand.

"Not too bad, Amonith. How 'bout yourself?"

"Pretty good. One of your crew members told me you wanted to see me."

"Yes. There are a couple of government officials on board who are going to oversee the shipment being unloaded on Obrah. From what I understand, they have some other government inspecting to do down on Obrah also. So, I was wondering if you could give them a lift. It would save me the time of prepping one of my shuttles I have in the other docking bay. I'm kind of on a tight schedule. We have to get the other pilot back to Yaraden. We've been having technical problems with the ship's lights. It's just been one of those weeks. So, if it wouldn't be a problem, I would appreciate the favor," Aarian said.

"Oh, that would be no problem at all. I wouldn't want the government officials to get upset at me because I don't shuttle them to Obrah. That's funny... Remember the time you used to haul Axithorps to Obrah. That government official wanted to see the load, so you opened the door. I never saw somebody turn so white. That Axithorp must have scared the shit out of him."

"Yeah, I don't think he ever asked to check someone's load again. If I didn't know what it was, I'd be scared too—seeing a large, green, ugly creature with sharp teeth staring down at me from the other side of the door."

Both men laughed for a moment.

"I'm sure these two inspectors are not as ignorant. They seem to be quite nice. So, I'll send them down when you're ready to leave," Aarian said.

"Okay. It was nice seeing you again. We'll see you later," Amonith said as he left the bridge.

"Yeah. Take it easy, Amonith."

Aarian turned on the intercom. "Tross, everything is okay. You can inform Shane and Ariel."

"Okay, Aarian, I'll do that," Tross said through the intercom.

Shane walked along a narrow service corridor searching for the problem with the ship's lights. He carried a tool box with him. Aarian had directed him to that area after the lights flickered once again.

Through the small rectangular holes in the metal grate floor, he could see the ship's other levels far below. The distant sound of the ship's engines echoed through the small passage. He noticed a panel located high above the walkway. A metal ladder led up to the area.

That must *be it*, he thought.

He slowly climbed the ladder, hanging onto his tool box. When he reached the upper area, he opened the panel. Many tiny strands of optical fibers spread across the inside of the panel. They led to several large bundles extending from the unit. Shane noticed a loose connection on one of the couplings. He repaired it and closed the panel.

Well, that should take care of the light problems.

Shane and Ariel sat in a lounge talking. They both held beverages in their hands.

"So, what type of work do you wanna do when you get to a safe planet?" Shane asked.

"I don't know. I think it would be fun to work in the clerical field," Ariel said.

"I think you would be very good at that," Shane said.

"Thanks."

Tross walked into the lounge and sat down next to them.

"You two can get a ride with the pilot back to Obrah. He thinks you are a couple of government officials who are here to inspect the shipment. So, when you land, make sure you inspect the shipment. Then find your way to a ship and get off the planet. Remember, Obrah might be on the border of the Galactic Government, but it is still in its jurisdiction. So, find a ship and get off the planet as soon as possible. If I were you, I wouldn't stop anywhere until I've passed at least two star systems. I think that will be far enough from the border to be safe from the Galactic Government," Tross said.

"Okay," Shane said. "Do you have any idea where we can find a ship down there?"

"You should be able to purchase one for a reasonable amount on Obrah," Tross said.

"I can't use my digital currency card. If I do, they'll know where I'm at," Shane said.

"That's not good. Well, you'll just have to do the best you can. We've done everything that we can possibly do," Tross said.

"Oh, I know, Tross. And I want to thank you for everything you've done. You've probably saved our lives. We'll do what we can to get off from Obrah," Shane said.

"And thanks for these uniforms you gave us. We sure wouldn't look like government officials in ripped pants and dirty clothes," Ariel said.

"You're welcome. The shuttle will be leaving shortly. So, if you are hungry, eat, and if you have to use the bathroom, use it. You should be in the docking bay in twenty minutes," Tross said.

"All right, we will. Thanks," Shane said.

"I hope you two get away with no problems. Bye," Tross said, shaking their hands. He left the room.

As the shuttle was being unloaded, Shane and Ariel inspected the shipment thoroughly. When the last skid settled onto the warehouse floor, they finished their task. One of the supervisors walked over to them.

"How does everything look?"

"Well, our results are confidential, but I will tell you that the food is edible. And your warehouse could use a bit of cleaning up. That's all I can tell you," Shane said.

"Oh," the man said, looking around the warehouse as if he did not expect them to observe that.

"Thank you for your time. We have a few more places to inspect, so we will be leaving," Ariel said.

"I'll see to it that the warehouse gets cleaned up. Thank you," the supervisor said.

Shane and Ariel left the warehouse and headed down a street. They walked through a few neighborhoods and stopped at an old, vacated building.

"I think that went well back there," Ariel said.

"Yes. I think so. Now, how are we going to find a ship?"

"We'll think of something," she said.

At that moment, an old man came around the corner of the old brick building. He had gray hair and a gray beard. As he rounded the corner, he avoided a few weeds that grew along the cracked bricks.

"Hi," the man said.

"Hi," Shane said.

"I overheard you saying that you needed a ship."

"You look familiar… You're the guy that gave me the picture with the scroll in it!"

"Yeah, that's me. Do you still have it?"

"Yes."

"Good. At least the government didn't find it. I was—"

"They know I have it. My life will never be the same," Shane said.

"No, I don't suppose it would. Mine won't either. They know I helped in it all. They've been after me all this time. It's very interesting that we both made it this far and bumped into each other," the man said.

"Yes, It *is* strange," Shane said. "Ariel, this is the man who gave me the scroll."

"The name is Moro. Moro Bassin. Nice to meet you, Ariel," he said.

"Nice to meet you too."

"So, do you two need a ride?" Moro asked.

"You have a ship?" Shane asked.

"Yeah."

"I thought you were stuck here on Obrah too," Shane said.

"No. I just stopped here at Misquee Shores to get something to eat. The government officials that have been chasing me know what I look like, but they don't know my name or account number. So, I can still use my digital currency card," Moro said.

"Let's hope they don't find a way to connect your looks with your account number," Shane said.

"I just happened to notice you walking down the street, so I thought I'd catch up with you and see what's up," Moro said.

"Well then, let's get going, shall we?" Shane said.

The three of them left the side of the building and headed down the street toward the downtown area.

"So, what are your plans now?" Shane asked Moro.

"Well, I'm definitely not going to help you search for the treasure. I think I'll just lay low for a while. You *are* going to continue to search for the treasure, aren't you?" Moro asked.

"Well, I really haven't even started yet. My first plan is to get off this planet and get out of the Galactic Government's jurisdiction. After that, I want to find a safe planet where Ariel can find a real job and start a new life for herself. Then I will go to see Shanda. Oh, how I miss

Shanda. Shanda and I will then go search for the treasure," Shane said. "That is, if she wants to go with me."

"So, you are going to need a ship. I tell you what, why don't I give you my ship so you can continue your quest?" Moro looked up at Shane and Ariel.

"Then, how are you going to find someplace to lay low for a while, without a ship?" Shane asked.

"You can drop me off at the same planet that you drop Ariel off at," Moro said.

"That sounds like a good idea, Moro. But I want to travel a few star systems out of the Galactic Government's jurisdiction before we find a planet for you two. You don't need to be too close to the border. And the planet must have some good job opportunities, or we'll have to find another one. Ariel needs a good job," Shane said.

"Yeah, that's true. I also need a job. One of the good things about being outside of the Galactic Government's jurisdiction is that we don't have to put up with that idiotic digital currency shit. We can just use regular merits, like old times. The merit system is more ethical than that trash," Moro said.

"Well, sometimes doing what's right and going against the flow is a hard thing to do, but we know deep down inside our hearts what is really right. It's too bad we have to experience persecution because of what we believe and how we feel. The whole galaxy can think they are doing what's right, but those few that know the truth are the one's who are right. The whole galaxy is wrong," Shane said.

"Wrong about what?" Ariel asked.

"You see, Ariel, they killed your parents. Look how your life has been because of the government. If people don't follow their corrupt rules, they get persecuted. None of us like the digital currency system. I used it, but I didn't agree with it. If I had to do over again, I would have never used it. It is wrong. They don't need to know what people buy or when and where they buy it. They don't need to know how many credits someone has in their account. They don't need to know where people are at all times. And they definitely don't need to keep an inventory of every person in the galaxy—or in their jurisdiction. They are evil people. They think they are right, but they're not. Take religion, for instance. They want everyone to be atheists, like them. They persecute people who love God. I used to be a very cruel person, myself. I used to hang with space gangs and terrorize innocent people.

I'm just thankful I'm not like that any longer. I have really changed over the last couple of years. I'm not perfect, but I know what's right. Look, we are being chased because of a treasure that we know about. Why do they want to kill us for it? I think this treasure is going to reveal a weakness in the Galactic Government. That is why they want it so badly," Shane said.

Silence followed as they continued to walk toward the spaceport shipyards of downtown Misquee Shores. The surrounding houses slowly faded as they mixed with the buildings of the business district. Misquee Shores was the most populated town on the planet. Obrah was discovered only one hundred years before. Shane gazed at the gray clouds that quickly proceeded from the north.

"It looks like it's gonna rain," Shane said.

"Yeah, we better hurry," Moro said.

Their walk became a quick pace as they entered the downtown area. They passed several people that were hurrying to finish their shopping before it started to rain.

"It looks like it's already raining over that way," Ariel said, pointing to the north.

Minutes later, they felt the rain. Cold drops poured down hard and fast. The clear scenery of downtown suddenly became a hazy shade of light gray. The long rain drops bounced off the concrete as they hit. Shane, Ariel, and Moro ran toward the shipyards.

Shane saw a large building on their right. "Is that the spaceport?"

"That's it," Moro said.

It took a few minutes to reach the building. They dashed underneath a canopy at the spaceport's entrance. Shane opened the door and they entered the building. They walked down a long corridor that led to the rear of the building. Several offices were on either side of the corridor. When they reached the end of the corridor, Moro signed out and waited for clearance. Shane and Ariel stood at the door looking at the rain pound off the spaceships.

"You are cleared for takeoff," the man behind the desk said. "Be careful. Until you're in space, visibility will be near zero."

"Okay, thanks," Moro said, walking over to where Shane and Ariel stood.

"This is the only spaceport that I've ever seen with a shipyard instead of an enclosed docking area," Shane said.

The man behind the desk looked at Shane. His eyes fixed on Shane for several seconds. "Aren't you the guy on the *Galaxy's High Degree of Wanted Criminals.* I saw you on television. You killed seven government officials. I'm calling security!" the man said.

"Don't believe everything you hear on television," Shane said.

"I think we better get out of here," Moro said, opening the door.

Moro led them toward his ship. They ran through the cold rain and came to a stop at the ship entrance. Moro opened the door and they went inside.

"Get fastened in; this is going to be a quick takeoff," Moro said, heading for the controls.

Shane and Ariel sat in a couple of chairs behind Moro. Ariel looked around the small ship. She noticed many objects lying about the ship's interior. Tools, clothes, and many other things were scattered about. She focused her attention on Shane when he looked at her.

"I am getting really pissed off. The government must have told the media to put me on television. And for something I *didn't even do.* They're making me look bad to a lot of people who don't know the truth. It *makes* me want to kill seven government officials, but I won't stoop to their level of scum. The only way I'd kill anybody is in self-defense," Shane said.

"I know you don't want to hurt anyone, Shane. They didn't tell people the truth because it would make them look bad. They don't even pay bounty hunters, they just have people who don't know the difference do it for free. Cheer up, Shane. Things will get better," Ariel said with a smile.

"I hope so," he said, smiling back at her.

Moro started the ship and several displays came to life. With a sudden force, they lifted from the shipyards. In the midst of all the action, Shane prayed, asking God for help. It had been a long time since Shane prayed. It felt good. He stared at the rain pounding at the observation window. As they soared through the atmosphere, the gray clouds became darker. Black clouds replaced the gray ones. Lightning flashed all around them. Sounds of thunder echoed through the ship. They felt the ship shift from the turbulent winds. Soon, the rain stopped and it became quiet. The darkness of space replaced the black clouds. Distant stars brightened the darkness. Moro set the ship for lightspeed.

"Can this thing go faster than lightspeed?" Shane asked.

"No. The engine has a governor on it," Moro said.

"Electronics…my specialty!" Shane said.

"There is a servicing panel in the rear of the ship to your left," Moro said.

"I see it."

Shane grabbed a tool from the floor and pried the panel from the wall. He looked inside. He saw the front part of the ship's engines. The engine governor was located below the cooling tubes.

"Do you have any small jumpers?" Shane asked.

"There should be some in that box behind Ariel," Moro said.

"Oh, okay."

Shane found the jumpers and returned to the opening in the wall. He reached down past the cooling tubes and connected a jumper onto a terminal. He connected the other end to the ship's master engine control unit. After making some small component adjustments, he connected a couple more jumpers to a different terminal and spliced them into the system.

"Okay. You should be able to go a little faster now. Oops, I just dropped a wrench straight down into the cargo hold," Shane said.

Moro made a few adjustments and the ship picked up speed.

"Well?" Shane asked.

"Now we're at one point seven times lightspeed," Moro said.

"Cool," Shane said, sitting back down in his chair.

"So, once we're dropped off on a planet, do you think you can handle this ship?" Moro asked.

"Oh, yeah. The only ship that I can't fly is one made by the Thraxians. With that alien technology, who could? How long did that race rule in the First Tiffan Siram Empire? I think it was something like two thousand two hundred and three years," Shane said.

"Yeah, something like that. It's a strange galaxy," Moro said.

"That's for sure."

The ship grew silent. The humming of the ship's engines was the only sound. Cosmic blue space dust drifted past the observation window with a swift motion. They passed several moonlets of ice as they entered a star system.

"Wake me up when we get about two star systems from here," Shane said.

"Sure thing," Moro said.

Shane looked at Ariel who was already sleeping. He closed his eyes and fell asleep.

• • •

Moro settled the ship firmly onto the ground. The city of Wintress lay before them. Its lights brightened the night sky. It was a city that never shut down—not even for the night. In comparison with Metrocity, Wintress was twice as large in size and three times the size in population. If there was anywhere outside of the Third Tiffan Siram Empire's jurisdiction that had plenty of job opportunities, it was Wintress. Shane saw the multitude of buildings densely spread as far as the eye could see. Wintress was not the only major city on Zenbat Oddnu IV. There were many other cities across the planet. One democratic government was in power for the entire planet. Shane, Ariel, and Moro stared out the ship's observation window.

"So, how are we going to work this?" Shane asked.

"Well, Ariel and I can look around in the morning and see if there are any job opportunities around this part of the city. We can sleep in the ship until we find jobs and save enough merits to rent our own apartments. You shouldn't have to stay here for more than a week, Shane," Moro said.

"I wonder if I can get a job in the clerical field," Ariel said.

"Oh, I'm sure you can find a clerical job in this city with no problem," Shane said.

"I wonder what type of job I can find," Moro said.

"What did you do before?" Ariel asked.

"I was a star crystal miner in the Rytoorian Asteroid Mass," he said.

"I don't think they'll have anything like that here," Shane said.

"I don't either," Moro said.

"Well, shall we go outside and take a look around?" Ariel asked.

"Sure. Why not?" Shane said.

They opened the ship door and went outside. The night air was chilly. Shane stood in front of the ship and looked around at the city. No one seemed to be out and about in the immediate vicinity. Shane noticed small pebble stones on the ground all around the area. Moro noticed him looking at the stones.

"Zenbat Oddnu IV used to be an ocean world millions of years ago. It dried up. That's what all these pebble stones are from," Moro said.

"Really? How did you know that?" Shane asked.

"I used to study all the populated planets of the galaxy. There are some interesting ones, I'll tell you," he said.

"I'll bet."

"Well, I think it's a little bit cold to be standing out here," Ariel said. "I'm going back in the ship."

"Yeah, it is a little bit cold out here. Let's get back inside," Shane said.

After returning to the ship, they talked to each other until they fell asleep. In the morning, Ariel and Moro left to look for jobs while Shane slept. As the sun crept higher in the sky, Shane woke to find Ariel and Moro gone. While they searched for jobs, Shane straightened up the inside of the ship. It was quite a mess. He folded Moro's clothes and put them in a pile behind a metal crate. The tools were next. He picked up all the tools scattered across the ship floor and put them in the tool box behind Ariel's chair. He looked inside the refrigerator and saw an ale. He grabbed it. As he drank the ale, he looked around the ship and told himself that it was clean enough. He sat down and looked at the metal crate behind Moro's clothes. Shane walked over to the crate and opened it. To his surprise, it contained several laser pistols and two laser rifles. Closing the lid, he took another drink of his ale and sat down again. He pulled the treasure document out from his pocket and observed it.

What did I get myself into? he thought.

He put the document back into his pocket and stared at the ship wall for several minutes. There was absolutely nothing for him to do sitting in the ship.

This has got to be the most boring situation, he thought.

After finishing his ale, he went outside. As he looked at the surrounding buildings, his thoughts turned toward Shanda. He missed her so much. He hoped she would not be angry with him for being away so long. If she was, she had every right to be. He was so angry with himself. Tears started flowing down his face. He did not want to be in his current situation. He wanted to be with Shanda. He wanted to take her in his arms and fly off to a remote planet. He wiped the tears from his eyes as he saw Ariel and Moro approaching in the distance.

"You two have been gone all day. How did you do?" Shane asked.

"I found a clerical job, like I wanted to!" Ariel said.

"I found a job doing inventory control. And we made some arrangements with a hotel manager. He agreed to let us stay there until we find our own places," Moro said.

"That's great," Shane said.

"Oh, and I overheard several people talking about something very interesting," Moro said.

"What?" Shane asked.

"I guess Straton is not the head of the Galactic Government anymore. There's a new leader named Boris Anathor. He changed the name of the government to the Third Tiffan Siram Empire. And the government and the Universal Expanse Church have merged together and become one. Now they plan on expanding their borders. They'll not only have power in their current jurisdiction, the entire Tiffan Siram Galaxy will be under their control. There will be no more free territory. I don't know when all this will take place, but someone has to do something about it. I guess there are some churches that oppose this merge. They think it is totally unrighteous. Everyone that I heard talking about it seems to be against it also. Boy, Shane, what are we going to do?" Moro asked.

"The Universal Expanse Church is the largest denomination here outside the Third Tiffan Siram Empire's jurisdiction. If they join the Third Tiffan Siram Empire, it will certainly not be an impossibility for them to control the entire Tiffan Siram Galaxy. I think we all better start doing a lot more praying. God does answer prayers. Remember, he *is* all-powerful. I don't see how the UEC can call itself a church. It became evil and twisted," Shane said.

"That's for sure. The people I heard talking, said they were afraid the church and government would execute them for not wanting to be part of the new system," Ariel said.

"It looks like that's what it's gonna come to," Shane said.

"Well, Shane, I don't know how long it will be before this new system reaches its way to Zenbat Oddnu IV, but you are right. All we can do is pray. We are at God's mercy. At least we have a name here, instead of a number. For now…"

"So, I guess I should be on my way to see Shanda," Shane said.

"Here is the address of the hotel we are staying at," Ariel said, handing Shane a business card. "We'll have the hotel manager keep our new addresses on file once we get our own places. So, if you ever come back, go to the hotel and ask for our addresses."

"Well then, I guess I'm off," Shane said.

He shook Moro's hand. Ariel hugged him tight.

"Thanks so much, Shane. You've changed my life," she said, a tear rolling down her cheek.

"You two take care now," Shane said. "Here, let me get your clothes."

"Oh, and can you grab me one of my laser pistols in that metal crate?" Moro asked.

"Sure."

Shane went inside the ship and took a laser pistol out of the metal crate. He picked up Moro's clothes and brought them both outside.

"Here you go," he said, handing them to Moro.

"Thanks. If you need an anti-gravitational transport, there is one in the cargo hold of the ship."

"Okay. Bye now," Shane said.

"Bye," Ariel and Moro said simultaneously.

"Hey, Moro, what is the name of your ship?" Shane asked.

"She's called *Star Crystal*…for what I used to mine," Moro said.

"Well, thanks for letting me use *Star Crystal*," he said.

"It's the least I could do after dragging you into this mess. Good luck, Shane," Moro said.

Shane went inside the ship and started its engines. Ariel and Moro stepped back from the ship to a safe distance and watched it slowly lift into the sky. Soon, it was just a black dot against the white clouds.

Chapter Eight

Emperor Boris Anathor sat in front of a computer screen. He gathered information on Shane Aslat. The outlaw was not going to get away with The Lost Scroll. Perhaps he could even lead the Third Tiffan Siram Empire to the treasure himself. Boris's mind raced as he searched Shane's files. He noticed the screen reveal several requests for permits to fly out of the Third Tiffan Siram Empire's jurisdiction to the planet Myrath. The reason stated by Shane: to see his girlfriend. A smile spread across Boris's lips. He rubbed his beard.

Myrath!

Shanda sat on a soft cushioned couch in Emperor Tulli's concubine chambers. She was alone in the room. The other women were down in the courtyard eating lunch. Shanda liked the peace and quiet. Being alone gave her time to think. She stared at the arm of the couch, collecting her thoughts. She thought of the dreadful situation that she was in. She thought of the freedom that she no longer had. She thought of Shane Aslat. And she prayed. It had been a long morning, and she was very tired. Her eyelids felt very heavy. She kept dozing off until, finally, she fell asleep.

Suddenly, the concubine chambers door burst open. Shane rushed in and found Shanda sleeping on the couch. He grabbed her arm and pulled her to her feet. With awesome surprise, she called out his name. Shane led her out of the room and toward the exit. Without warning, one of Emperor Tulli's knights drove his staff straight through Shane's chest. He doubled over and fell to the marble floor.

"No!" Shanda screamed.

She sat straight up on the couch, a cold sweat covering her forehead. Her head was racing. She looked around the concubine chambers and sighed.

Oh, man…what a terrible dream, she thought.

One of Emperor Tulli's aides walked into the room. "Is everything okay? I heard a scream," he said.

"Oh, everything is just totally frickin' peachy. Why don't you just get out of my face?"

"Now, now, let's not crack under pressure," the man said.

Shanda stood up from the couch, her hand clenched into a fist. "I'm gonna crack your face with pressure. Now, go!" she said.

The man turned around and left. Shanda put both hands on her forehead. She could not handle the stress any longer. She was surprised the burst of rage did not happen sooner.

"I just want to go home," she said to herself.

The distant planet of Myrath stood out against the blackness of space. Shane adjusted several controls as the ship approached the planet. He was so anxious to see Shanda. He wanted to give her the biggest hug. His thoughts about her could not stop. As he entered the atmosphere of Myrath, he thought about the last time he was there. It was an old-era planet. They used horses, not AGTs. They used swords, not laser weapons. To Shane, it was a little backwards, but he liked it. It was not very often that a ship landed on Myrath. There was not even a spaceport.

Here we are, Shane thought.

He saw the town of Almoss through the observation window. He settled the ship next to Shanda's house. When the ship came to rest on the firm ground, Shane sighed and unfastened his seat belt. He stood up and headed for the ship door. Shane squinted when he reached the outside. The sun was very bright, compared to the low illumination in the ship. He walked toward the house and knocked. There was no answer. He tried again. Finally, he opened the door and went inside. She was not in the kitchen, bedroom, nor bathroom.

This is strange, Shane thought.

He went back outside. There, he found several people staring at his ship. They shifted their attention to Shane and then back to the ship. One of Shanda's neighbors walked up to Shane.

"Do you know Shanda?" Shane asked.

"Yes. I'm her neighbor. She's been gone for quite some time. You must be Shane. She always talks about you. But she hasn't been around here for about two weeks. Last week, her boss came to find her. I told him the same thing. There is a rumor going around that Emperor Tulli abducted her. She's not the only one that has ever just disappeared. I'm pretty sure he has concubine chambers where he keeps all those women. Emperor Tulli thinks he owns this town. His men are always starting trouble down at the intoxication joint," the woman said, gazing at the Tulli Castle high above Almoss.

Shane followed her gaze with his own eyes. There it was—the towering castle atop the mountain. It seemed to reach the clouds. Suddenly, Shane was overcome by the situation. He felt sadness, fear, and worry all at the same time.

"Thanks for the information," he said, heading for his ship.

He sat at the controls staring into nothingness.

What am I going to do? he asked himself. *I never noticed that castle the last time I was here.*

He came to the conclusion that he should go to a distant town and land the ship. He did not want Emperor Tulli to get suspicious if the ship stayed in Almoss. He started the ship and it lifted from the ground.

I'll go to the town of Thisilia and make my way back here by horse. Yeah, that'll work, Shane thought.

Shane landed his ship in the town of Thisilia. After he had turned off the ship's engines, Shane opened the box located behind his seat. He grabbed two laser pistols and a laser rifle. Fortunately, the laser pistols were small enough to fit in his pockets. He slung the laser rifle over his shoulder. Before he left the ship, he took a bottle of ale from the refrigerator. The bottle fit nicely in his upper pocket. He left the ship and locked the door. He thought about using the anti-gravitational transport in the cargo hold that Moro had mentioned, but the forest was too thick between Thisilia and the Tulli Castle. Hopefully no one from the Tulli Empire was in the town. Even if there was, they would not know what Shane was doing there.

The sun was shining, however there was a chill in the air. Shane walked down a small street which seemed to be the main street of the town. A few people could be seen outside, attending to their tasks. Shane walked to a large building where horses were rented and sold. He opened the door and walked inside. It was an older building. Large stains of some sort covered the walls. There was dust and cobwebs on most of the furnishings. The paint on the walls was chipped and cracked. Behind the counter sat an old man with gray hair.

"It's not every day we get a ship from off-world landing in Thisilia. What can I do for you, sir?"

"I would like to rent a horse. I have to ride to Almoss," Shane said.

"Well, you better get a horse that knows how to swim real good, because if you go by land, it'll take a lot longer," the old man said.

"What do you mean?" Shane asked.

"Come hear. I'll show you on the map," the man said, walking over to a map on the counter.

Shane looked at the dusty map.

"See, we are right here," the man said, pointing to a particular spot on the map. "And here is Almoss. If you go across this portion of the Slave Sea, it would be a lot faster than going around the bay."

"Yeah," Shane said.

"If you go over to the docks, you might find a sailor who will bring you across. In fact, I know one of the sailors. I don't know if he is out on the sea right now or not, but if he's docked, tell him that I sent you to him. People call him Ironclad. And my name is Morrison."

"Okay. How do I know what ship is his?" Shane asked.

"It's a very large ship with white sails. It's the only large ship in Thisilia."

"All right. And what type of terrain will I be experiencing on the other side of the sea?" Shane asked.

"There will be forest and mountains on the other side," Morrison said, pointing to the map. "And if you would have proceeded around the bay on horse, you would have seen many wooded lands and forest."

"I see," Shane said. "Well, thank you so much for the information. It will be very helpful to me."

"No problem whatsoever. Take it easy now," Morrison said.

"Yeah, you too," Shane said as he walked to the door.

"By the way, why don't you just fly to Almoss in your ship?" Morrison asked.

"It's a long story. Can you keep an eye on it for me, though?" Shane asked.

"Sure. That would be no problem at all. Take care now."

"Yeah. See ya," Shane said as he left the building.

Shane walked down the street toward a small intersection where he turned right and headed for the docks. He saw an old, large sail ship at the docks along with a few smaller ones.

That must be it, he thought.

The Slave Sea was beautiful. Shane could see several birds flying through the air with such precision. As he walked along the old wooden dock, he peered to his right and noticed the beige sand with tall grass extending from it. To his left, he noticed many white stones that had washed ashore and settled on top of the sand. The dock extended out into the water to half the length of the ship. There were several crewmen on the docks attending to various tasks. Shane saw an older man moving some ropes at the end of the dock. He wore a blue hat that matched his blue outfit.

"Hi, there," Shane said to the man.

The man turned around. "Oh, hi. Can I help you with something?" the man asked.

"Yeah. Do you know where I can find a man named Ironclad?" Shane asked.

The man looked at the laser rifle slung over Shane's shoulder. "Why do you want to know?"

Shane saw that he was looking at the rifle. "My name is Shane Aslat. I'm not here to hurt anyone. I just need a ride across the sea toward Almoss. I was sent by a man named Morrison. I'm from off-planet. And for certain reasons, I cannot fly my ship into Almoss," Shane said.

"Oh, I see, Mr. Aslat. I am Ironclad. Morrison sent you, huh?"

"Yeah."

"Well, I'll charge you fifty merits for the ride," Ironclad said.

"That's going to be a problem. I don't have any merits. But I brought an extra laser pistol that you can have," Shane said.

"A laser pistol? You've got yourself a deal, Aslat. I have an old projectile pistol, a sword, a dagger, and a staff, but I never thought I would own a laser pistol. I've never even seen one. I've only heard about them. Can you show me how it works?"

"Sure," Shane said, pulling it out of his pocket. "This is the power switch. When it is off, it won't fire. This is the trigger switch. And if this red light starts flashing, then something is wrong with the superconductor infinite power supply, and you will probably only have several shots left. Theoretically, they are made to work forever, but realistically, they go bad sometimes. I've only seen two go bad, though. Some laser weapons have different options too. Go ahead, shoot it."

"Okay," Ironclad said, taking the pistol from Shane's hand.

He pointed it into the water and pulled the trigger. A blue beam came from the pistol.

"Well?" Shane looked at Ironclad.

"I like this. Are you ready to sail?"

"Whenever you are," Shane said.

"All aboard! We're ready to sail," the captain yelled.

Shane followed Ironclad up the steep incline crossing between the dock and the ship. As they climbed aboard the large ship, Shane noticed stains in the old wooden ship's side. When they reached the deck, the large, off-white sails caught Shane's attention as a gust of wind blew into them. Ironclad led Shane to the bridge.

"Make yourself comfortable here. I have to see if my crewmen have everything ready," Ironclad said.

"Oh, okay," Shane said.

Ironclad left the room. Shane surveyed the bridge with awe. There were several windows overlooking the bow of the ship. Fixed in front of the windows was the wooden captain's wheel. Shane sat in the captain's chair. A large compass was fixed next to the window. There were four round life preservers hanging on the wall. Two lanterns hung on either side of the room. There was extra rope in one corner. Behind Shane, there were two doors. One revealed Ironclad's bedroom chamber, the other was a storage closet.

Soon, Ironclad returned to the bridge to find Shane sleeping in his captain's chair. "Mr. Aslat, wake up."

Shane's eyes opened in surprise. "Oh, I'm sorry. I guess I'm a little tired."

"You're welcome to one of the extra crew beds, if you want to go to sleep for a while," Ironclad suggested.

"Oh, no. That's okay. Thanks for the offer, though. So, is this the largest port on the Slave Sea?"

"No, we are actually one of the smallest. There are a few ports to the south that are pretty large. Those towns have many industrial areas," Ironclad said.

"How long will it take to get to my destination?" Shane asked.

"A few hours. You are invited to have lunch with me and my crewmen later. We are having fish," Ironclad offered.

"That sounds good. Thanks. Do you mind if I walk the deck for a while?" Shane asked.

"No, not at all. Be my guest," Ironclad said.

Shane left the bridge and walked out onto the deck. A few crewmen could be seen here and there. Shane tried to find a place where no one was around. He wanted to relax and enjoy the view. He needed some time alone. The deck boards creaked as he walked along side the ship's railing. Close to the stern of the ship, Shane found a quiet place to relax. He sat on a wooden crate and opened the ale that he had put in his pocket earlier. Taking a drink, he looked up. The sea was beautiful. The distant sound of splashing water hitting the side of the ship made Shane very tired. He fell asleep.

After lunch, Shane and Ironclad stood at the bow of the ship. They peered across the waters to the land beyond.

"There's your destination." Ironclad pointed to the distant shore.

Shane moved to the other side of one of the ship's stays to get a better look.

"That looks like a nice expanse of beach," Shane said.

"Yeah, but there are many jagged rocks through there. We can't bring the *Maritime Maiden* that close. One of my crewmen will have to bring you ashore with one of the small boats."

"So, why do they call you Ironclad?" Shane asked.

A husky laugh filled the bow. "It all started from a card game. All my buddies thought I was going to put iron plates on the sides of *Maritime Maiden.* I *did* talk about doing it, but I decided not to. They started calling me Ironclad after that. That was back when there was tension between Thisilia and Port Fae. There was fierce competition between the shipping companies of the two towns. A few of the captains put iron plates on the sides of their ships. Three ships were sunk in the shipping lanes of Port Fae."

"Oh. That sounds familiar. My parents died in a space war similar to that," Shane said.

"I'm sorry. Yeah, wars don't make much sense to me… We'll be there soon. I'll go prep the small boat for you," Ironclad said.

"Okay."

Shane stood on the sandy beach. He waved to the crewman that dropped him off. The small boat slowly made its way back through the jagged rocks and headed for the massive ship. The tall masts of the *Maritime Maiden* seemed to touch the sky. As Shane stood and watched the small boat depart, a large wave splashed against one of the rocks causing a refreshing mist to fall upon him. With one last look, he turned his back to the sea and faced the forest. There were various types of trees along the beach. Shane headed for them. As the sand faded away, it was replaced with leaves and twigs. He made his way through the forest until he came to the foot of the mountain. There, he rested for a while before continuing. As he sat on a large stone next to a tree, his thoughts returned to Yaraden. He remembered the troops chasing him through the rain. He remembered the crash landing just before that. Suddenly, a deer ran by him at lightning speed.

"Wow!" he exclaimed.

He stood up from the large stone and watched the deer fade into the distant trees. Thinking of Shanda's rescue, Shane looked up the wooded mountain and headed in that direction. After an hour of climbing, he saw the towering castle. It loomed overhead like a dark dragon. An eerie feeling came over Shane.

I have to hurry…dusk is here. Soon, it will be dark, Shane thought.

He continued up the mountain.

In the night's darkness, Shane vaguely saw one of the castle doors. As he approached the door, he retrieved the laser rifle from his shoulder. The door was open.

Why should they lock the doors? No one in their right mind would come here by choice, anyway. I guess that means I'm insane, Shane thought.

The inner passage was dark and cold. Shane made his way through a series of small corridors to a large weapons room. There was no one in the room. A wide assortment of swords, shields, daggers, staves, and projectile guns was in the room. There were also many chain whips and other strange looking weapons. Shane considered gathering a few of the weapons for himself to ensure extra protection. He decided to only grab a dagger. It fit nicely through the loops on the outside of his right boot. He noticed two other doors in the room. One led to an outer passage. The other led to a storage closet. Shane quickly took the weapons in the room and put them into the storage closet. He then wedged the door so it would be very difficult to open. He hoped no one heard the noise he made. Continuing into the outer passage, Shane prowled around every corner. He roamed around the castle until he came across a man in one of the rooms adjacent to the courtyard. He entered the room.

"Who on Myrath are you?" the man asked, a surprised expression across his face.

Shane pointed the laser rifle at him. "Show me the way to the concubine chambers. Get up off the chair and show me, now, before I shoot you."

The man looked around the room for a weapon. There was none. Shane lowered the rifle's power to stun and shot the man. He fell backwards in his chair. A few seconds later he stirred in the chair.

"Are you going to show me?" Shane asked.

"Yes, yes…right this way," the man said, trying to keep himself from shaking with nervousness.

Shane followed the man out into the corridor. They passed the courtyard and went up a stairway. The stairway ended at a large circular room. From there, the man led him up another stairway. Shane thought he saw someone out of the corner of his eye. Suddenly, an arrow pierced him in the shoulder. He grimaced with pain as he grabbed his shoulder. The man ahead of him turned around and saw what had happened. He kicked Shane in the ribs and sent him down the stairs to the floor of the circular room. A tear came from Shane's eye and fell to the cold floor. It was the very same spot where Shanda's tears fell just weeks earlier. Shane pointed the laser rifle toward the man on the stairs and pulled the trigger. This time the power was on maximum. Two other men quickly approached him. One of them had a bow and a bag of arrows. Shane whipped the rifle around toward them. With no warning, intense, blue streaks of laser fire illuminated the passage. The two men fell to the floor. Shane stood up and looked down at his wounded shoulder. With loud, painful cries that echoed throughout the castle passage, Shane broke the head off the arrow and slid it out of his shoulder. A trail of blood trickled down the sleeve of his jacket.

"Ahhh!" He slammed his fist against the stairway railing as he tried to control the pain.

Stepping over the man beside him, Shane continued up the winding stairs. He stopped at a fork in the stairway. A smaller stairway turned off to the right. He continued on the main stairway. It ended at a large room with many windows. As he approached one of them, he could see the lights of Almoss far below the mountain. There were a few other doors that led off the large room. Shane decided to try the other stairway. He left the room and headed down the stairs to the fork. As he headed up the other stairway, he glanced down at the men that he had shot earlier, their bodies slumped on the floor of the circular landing. This winding stairway was much longer than the other. It ended at a large room where two knights stood at a far door. When Shane entered the room, the knights looked at him and then at each other. They drew their staves and charged Shane. As they passed the fountain in the center of the room, Shane shot them. They fell to the marble floor with a thud, their metal staves rolling across the room. Shane looked at the large doors beyond the fallen knights. He walked toward the entrance of the throne room.

What did I get myself into? he thought as he gazed at the immense pillars in the corners of the room.

He opened the doors and surveyed the throne room. Across the room, Shane saw an old man sitting on a throne. There were a few other people in the room. When they saw the doors fly open, their attention was drawn to the entrance. With a quick flick of the wrist, Emperor Tulli pulled a lever on the side of his throne. Suddenly, a portcullis fell from the entrance door, blocking Shane's way. Spikes on the bottom of the portcullis penetrated several centimeters into the marble floor. It would be impossible to lift. Shane had a better idea. He cut through the metal bars with his laser rifle by firing at each of the bars. The cut-out fell to the floor with a loud, metallic echo. Emperor Tulli and the others looked at Shane in disbelief.

"Who are you?" the emperor asked as he stood from his throne.

The men with Emperor Tulli drew their swords. Shane shot all three of them. The men fell to the floor, their swords making a metallic noise as they hit the marble floor. As Shane pointed the laser rifle at the emperor, the emperor covered his face and shouted.

"You have my woman here and I want her back. I'm willing to destroy this entire castle, if I have to. Show me where she is, now, or I'll kill you and find her myself," Shane shouted with an insane expression on his face.

The emperor slowly stepped down from the throne pedestal. He took too long for Shane's patience. Laser fire quickly destroyed the throne. The emperor quickened his pace.

"You'll hang for this…just as soon as the cards are in my hand," Emperor Tulli said.

"No, I don't think I will. I don't feel that it's my destiny to die in this scum ridden castle of yours. And I don't have to put up with your mouth," Shane said, raising his rifle.

"No don't shoot. If she's here, she's in there," he said, pointing toward a door to the left of Shane.

"Thanks," Shane said, pulling the trigger.

Emperor Tulli dropped to the cold floor. Shane opened the door to his left. Inside, he saw several women dressed in lingerie. Some of them were nude. He saw Shanda. Shanda saw him.

"Shane!" She stood up from the padded floor and ran to him. "Oh, Shane. You came for me! Thank God."

"Shanda, are you all right?" Shane asked as they hugged each other tight.

"Yes, I'm fine," she said, holding back tears.

"Come on, sweetheart, we have to leave here quickly. If any of you other women want to leave this place, now's the time," Shane said as he put his arm around Shanda.

All the women stood up and waited for Shane. The nude ones quickly grabbed their garments and put them on. Shane led them out the door and into the throne room. As they passed through the room, the women gazed at the emperor and his men on the floor. Shane took the extra laser pistol from his pocket and handed it to Shanda.

"It's a good thing you picked tonight to break in here; most of the emperor's men are out investigating a ship that landed in Almoss earlier," Shanda said.

"That would be my ship. When will they return?" Shane asked.

"I'm not sure. The emperor was up waiting for them. Is your ship still there?"

"No, but we have to hurry," Shane said as he quickened his pace.

They made their way through the castle and down to the entrance. There was very little resistance. After they exited the castle, Shane led them to a secluded path near a few trees, some distance from the castle.

"Okay…I have a plan for Shanda and I. If I were you women, I would go back to Almoss tonight. Get your lives straightened out the best you can. And find some kind of protection so this type of thing doesn't happen again. But whatever you do, don't take the main trail that leads up the mountain to the castle. If possible, try another route through the forest. Because if the emperor's men return and you are on the main trail, then they'll see you," Shane said.

"I know another way down to Almoss. My sister and I used to sneak up here when we were kids. It's over there," one of the women said, pointing toward the dark forest.

"Thanks so much for rescuing us. We are very grateful," another of the women said.

The rest of the women followed in their gratitude.

"You are all very welcome. Good luck on your journey. Be careful," Shane said.

The women departed into the eerie forest. Shane looked at Shanda and smiled.

"Let's go," he said.

"We have a lot to catch up on, don't we?"

"Yes, we sure do," Shane said, making his way through a few small trees.

"Why have you stayed away for a year, Shane. Don't you know I love you? Do you still love me? I've missed you so much. I thought you didn't care about me anymore," she said as tears rolled down her cheeks.

They stopped by a small hill and Shane hugged her. "Oh, Shanda, I love you so much. Believe me, I've missed you too."

Shane helped Shanda down the hill. He then jumped down himself.

"I have so much to tell you, Shanda," Shane said.

"Well, can you tell me as soon as we get to a safe place?"

"You're right. We better get to my spaceship as soon as possible."

"Yeah, before they find it first. Where is it?" Shanda asked.

"It's in Thisilia. I sailed across the bay in a sail ship. The captain gave me a ride in exchange for a laser pistol. But to get back to Thisilia, we have to go around the bay. There is much forest to go through," Shane said.

"I don't think they'll look for your ship as far as Thisilia."

"Let's hope not."

They continued walking down the mountain through the dark forest. A warm mist of rain started falling from the night sky. As soon as they reached the foot of the mountain, they walked along the shore of the bay until the terrain made it impossible to continue. The shore was blocked by many fallen trees and thick foliage. The trees that blocked the way were covered with a wet, slippery moss from the waves splashing upon them. Abruptly, the warm mist turned into a shower. They headed away from the shore, walking into the forest. Soon, the terrain became more manageable. The trees provided some shelter from the pouring rain. They worked their way through the thick trees and bushes. As they continued, the forest thinned out. There was more space to walk around trees.

"What is that ahead of us?" Shanda asked, looking through the hazy fog.

The moonlight revealed a strange scene ahead of them.

"It looks like an old mansion of some sort," Shane said.

As they came closer, Shane found that he was correct. There was an old, ragged mansion straight ahead of them. A graveyard set across from the mansion. A trail that separated the mansion from the graveyard led into the forest in either direction.

"This is spooky," Shanda said.

"Yeah. Some family must have lived here for years. There's at least fifteen to twenty tombstones here," Shane said.

As they walked past the foggy graveyard, Shanda held Shane's arm tight. They crossed the trail and headed for the mansion.

"It doesn't look like anyone's been living here for years. We should really get out of this rain. We're getting soaked," Shane said.

"Yes. I'm tired anyway," Shanda said.

"Well, we could stay here for the night and get some rest. That way, our clothes will have a chance to dry. We can continue in the morning," Shane said.

They looked at the three story mansion. Many of the boards were rotted. Several pieces of the upper levels were collapsed. Shane walked over to the front of the mansion. Shanda was right behind him. They went up a few stone steps and opened the front door. As they walked across the porch and into an old living room, the floorboards creaked with an eerie sound. They made their way past an old staircase that led to the second level. A brick fireplace was adjacent to the stairs. The ancient furnishings were rotted and covered with a strange moss. Shanda sneezed from the musty smell. As they made their way into the large dining room, Shane's foot fell through the rotted floorboards. He quickly grasped the wall next to him and pulled his foot from beneath the surface of the floor.

"Be very careful where you walk, Shanda."

A long table was centered in the dining room. It was covered with thick dust. A large chandelier hung from the ceiling. Several pieces of sharp wood extended through the ceiling from the collapsed floor above. A trickle of water started falling down from the holes above. The pouring rain could be heard on the old mansion roof. Two other doorways were in the dining room. One was impossible to reach because of the rotted floor boards. Any attempt to go in that particular direction would lead straight down to the cellar. The other door led to a kitchen. As they passed through the old kitchen, they saw numerous cobwebs strung along the cupboards and ceiling. Spiders crawled along a network of webs in the kitchen sink. A slimy mold covered the kitchen window. Shanda screamed as a mouse crawled across the floor in front of them.

"Let's get out of the kitchen," Shanda said. "This is sick."

Entering a short hallway, Shane quickly peered out a window as a flash of lightning struck a tree in the forest. It was immediately followed by a loud thunderous crash that made Shanda jump.

"My shoulder is starting to hurt very badly where that arrow went through," Shane said as he held his shoulder.

"Let me take a look," Shanda said.

"It's a little dark in here to see it," Shane said.

"You're right. But we have to take care of that as soon as possible, or it will become infected pretty badly."

"I am hungry too. Shanda, I feel so bad about killing those people back there in the castle. I was just trying to defend myself," Shane said.

"I know you were, Shane. I know you didn't mean to do it. But I think they probably deserved what they got."

"Shanda, back when I was in the Tyrris Militia, I hurt a lot of people. I feel very bad about that too. I wanna be a better person."

"Oh, Shane, I love you."

"I love you too, Shanda."

They continued down the hallway to where it ended at three doors. The doors revealed bedrooms. They chose the cleanest one and entered.

"This doesn't look too bad. I think we can get some rest here," Shane said.

"Yeah. We have a lot to talk about too," Shanda said.

The top blanket on the bed was a little dusty. Shane took it off the bed and set it aside. He then took the pillows and beat the dust out of them. They both lay down on the bed and sighed.

"Shanda, I know you've been through a lot lately. Are you *really* okay?" Shane asked.

She looked at Shane and smiled. Their eyes met for a long moment.

"I am now. Thank you for being my hero. With all those women from the concubine chambers, Emperor Tulli was sexually spent. Half the time, he couldn't get his cock hard," Shanda said.

"You're joking. Maybe you intimidated him with you're beauty. I'm just glad you're okay," Shane said.

She smiled. "I am so thankful that it's over."

"Oh, Shanda, I love you."

"I love *you*."

"I don't know where to begin, Shanda. I've also been through a lot in the last month. It all started when I needed some time off work. Business was a little slow in the electronics field, and I had a vacation coming anyway. So, I had them transfer my vacation pay to my account. Then I went on a vacation, traveling to a few of my favorite spots. Then I heard about this historical art festival on Selnaan. So, I went there and was looking through some ancient things from around the galaxy. Then this man came up to me and gave me this picture. He said there was something inside that would lead to a treasure. He was very persistent. So, I took the picture to my ship and opened the back of it. An old scroll fell out. I have it in my pocket. Then—"

"What does the scroll say?" Shanda asked.

"I'll get to that in a minute. Anyway, then a Galactic Government Trooper came to my ship and asked me about the picture. I thought, *Oh, what did I get myself into.* I knew the scroll was very important, so I quickly took off and headed into space. They followed me and shot my ship down. I crash landed on Yaraden. It was there that I met up with this harlot. Please don't think that we did anything together, because we didn't. She was very against the digital currency system. She didn't have an account in the computer. Her parents were killed by the government because they refused to join the new monetary system. She didn't want to be a harlot anymore. I told her that I had to leave the Galactic Government's jurisdiction very soon and that she was welcome to come with me. I told her there was a better life waiting for her on the outside of the government's jurisdiction. I know there are a few tyrants out here—like Tulli—but it sure beats the Galactic Government. Anyway, we hitched a ride on an old space freighter. I just happened to know the captain's partner. We used to hang around the intoxication joints together. He owed me a favor. Obrah is as far as he could take us, but it is right on the Galactic Government's border. On Obrah, we met up with the man that gave me the picture with the scroll in it. I guess he had been on the run too. We flew his ship out of the Galactic Government's jurisdiction and into freedom. I also found out that the Galactic Government put me on the *Galaxy's High Degree of Wanted Criminals* for killing some Galactic Government Troops. I don't know how they came up with that. I didn't kill any troops. So, then we found a nice planet for Moro and Ariel to live. Then we found out that the main leader of the Galactic Government had been killed. There is a new leader who is worse than the old one. He changed the name of the government from the Galactic Government to the Third Tiffan Siram Empire. Then the Third Tiffan Siram Empire and the Universal Expanse Church joined together. Now they are trying to dominate the entire galaxy. They are coming up with new religious laws. And they think they are doing the right thing. Then—"

"Aren't they doing the right thing?" Shanda asked.

"No. Not when they are forcing religion. It is something that must be a freedom of choice. I know God wouldn't want us to be forced to worship Him against our will. Next thing you know, the Third Tiffan Siram Empire and the Universal Expanse Church will be saying that their leader is God. They really want to manipulate the people. We can't let that happen. I feel like I am being pushed into finding this treasure. I really feel like God wants me to find it. Do you think I am exaggerating, Shanda?"

"No, I don't, Shane. When I was trapped in that castle, I felt that something big was about to take place. Somehow, I knew that you would rescue me. Now, here I am, caught up in the middle of it all. I can hardly believe that all this is happening around the galaxy. Oh, Shane, it is such a scary feeling," Shanda said.

"Yeah, it sure is. Moro gave me his ship to search for the treasure. I wanted you to come with me. So, I stopped at your house in Almoss. One of your neighbors suspected that you were a prisoner in the Tulli Castle. So, here I am!"

She smiled at him.

"Now, the scroll I have," Shane said as he pulled it out of his pocket, "is actually The Lost Scroll that we studied about in college. I can make most of it out. It was written by the Scyllian Clan of the planet Raatoris. It says that they discovered a treasure in the Namaas Forest on the planet. They built the Ojenis Temples in the forest to preserve the treasure in. I remember from college that the Namaas Forest covers approximately one third of the planet Raatoris. They built enormous statues outside of the Ojenis Temples. The only problem is that I don't know where this Raatoris is. I *do* know from college that it is an ancient planet where no one lives anymore. It was set aside as a memorial planet in ancient times. It is the planet where the First Tiffan Siram Empire was formed. I've been thinking about all the planet names that I know about. The only one that comes close to Raatoris is Toris. It is an old abandoned planet on the edge of the Tiffan Siram Galaxy. It is so remote that very few people know it exists. I found out about it back when I used to hang around in the intoxication joints."

"That has to be it," Shanda said.

"Yeah."

"I just have one question for you, Shane."

"What's that?"

"When you were on your vacation, why didn't you think about coming to see me?"

"Shanda, I wanted to, believe me. The government wasn't giving out permits to cross the border. I was denied several times. So, I was going to sneak across, but before I could, I was caught up in this treasure thing. But I don't want to leave you ever again, Shanda," Shane said, a tear rolling down his cheek.

"Oh, Shane, I love you."

"I love you too."

They hugged and held the embrace for several minutes. She noticed the necklace that she had given him long ago.

"You still have the necklace I gave you."

"Yeah. I always wear it," he said.

She gave him a warm smile.

"I think we should try to get some sleep," Shane said.

They relaxed on the bed and stared at the old ceiling.

An hour later, Shanda looked at Shane. "I can't sleep."

"Me neither. How about if I read you some poems?"

"Poems? From where?" Shanda asked.

"I have a little book that I purchased at the historical art festival back on Selnaan," Shane said, pulling out the book.

He opened it up and cleared his throat. "Remyw Yort was a legendary poet from years ago. His poetry moves people. It really touches hearts. Some of them are a little strange, however. This is some of his stuff. Okay, this is called *The Sands of Time:*

> We are conceived, we are born.
> Birth is so painful, yet so beautiful.
> We are so cute when we are young.
> We become beautiful men and women.
> The memories are so clear, yet so faint.
> There was sorrow, there was happiness.
> There was foolishness, there was wisdom.
> We have goals for the future.
> We have expectations of others.
> We are so independent, yet we rely on others.
> We are so poor, yet we are so rich.
> We are so rich, yet we are so poor.
> Our love is so sweet, yet so bitter.
> We age, yet time seems to stand still.
> The gray of our hair, the wrinkling of our skin,
> We know death is near. We are afraid.
> We focus on memories from our past.
> We grow old and frail.
> The memories are there again.
> We were such beautiful young creatures.
> We remember our childhood clearly now.
> One day we will be gone.
> We will be set free.
> Then we will roam the heavens.
> We must look to our lives…

It is not wrong to enjoy memories from the past.
But we should not dwell on them.
We should always look forward to the future.
We should look death in the face.
The next life has the potential to be much better.
It depends on who your heart belongs to.
We are afraid and we worry.
But we are only sinful humans;
What is to be expected?"

"That's very touching. Is there more?"
"Yeah. This one is called *Ineffective Life:*

In this ineffective life…we live.
This ineffective life isn't working.
There is so much pain.
People on the street, starving to death.
People with no home, taking their last breath.
People working for nothing, to get it all taken away.
People trying to survive, in this ending day.
Children with no parents, scared and all alone.
Children deprived of life, like a king without a throne.
Children yet not born, will they have a chance?
Children of tomorrow, need not a single glance.
We must help each other in this ineffective life.

"Here are some more. *Ancient Prophets:*

Satan will give his final commands.
Centuries of horror will age the lands.
Militia of death will roam the sands.
The fate of us all is in our own hands.
The prophets, they will be right.
Their visions, our own sight.
You must see the light.
All the evil, we must fight.
One thousand years of peace, you'll see,
All the divine, we'll be free.
To all the evil, this won't be.

You better be prepared, listen to me,
Apocalyptic prophecy.

"Futuristic Dreams:

Futuristic dreams, things that won't be,
There is another way, just wait and see.
Time…
Does it really exist?
Or is it an illusion?
An infinite voyage?
Phenomenal conceptions in our minds?
Frost upon our cortex?
Dust, itching at our brain?
Time, driving us insane?
Time…
Is it linear?
Or does it vary?
Are we free?
Are we living in a fantasy?
Or futuristic dreams?
No we're not!
It's as real as it seems!

"Life's Sorrow:

In this world we live,
Life and death are separated by nothing.
Life is so fragile.
Life is so delicate.
We live.
We die.
It's all around us.
But when it affects us, it's not the same.
It seems that the good die too early,
And the evil, not at all.
Perhaps that's an indication
That God wants His special people to be with Him.
When someone dies that you love,

It's so, so sad.
Life's sorrow…
When someone dies that you love,
A part of you dies too.
We're only made up of so many parts.
Life's sorrow is slowly killing us all.

"Reigning On You (Return of Thee):

The Emperor of all emperors
Is quite an Emperor.
Tyrannical emperors are dethroned.
But the sacrificial Emperor returns.
Then He reigns on you.
The divinity of the Most High
Is quite high.
The All-seeing Eye sees all.
The Ancient of Days owns time itself.
Reigning on you, the love will never cease.
Return of Thee, the feeling of endless peace.

"Oh, I didn't know this was in here. Harris Romison was a wise man. He had more words of wisdom than anyone in history. The following are words of wisdom taken from his *Wisdom Chronicles:*

'From the establishment of the imperium unto the present time, there have existed numerous occasions of the reduction of the freedom of the people of the galaxy from the gradual and calm intrusion of their rights by the government officials in power, than there has been by the intense and abrupt control by revolution. This cycle will continue. A force in power must deal with its subjects just as its officials would personally want to be dealt with. After all, they are their own subjects. Perhaps that is the problem.'

"Vincent Ryineos was known for his *Expeditionary Journals* from his travels throughout the galaxy. The following is an excerpt from one of the volumes of his *Expeditionary Journals:*

'For those who will never have the opportunity to leave their home world, I bring these illustrative writings. Imagine the mists drifting on the sands of an island seashore. Picture the continuous waves of an ocean world…Water creatures wondrously playing at the surface where the fresh air is cool and the wind is breezy.'

"Well, that's it. That's all that is in this little book," Shane said.

"It's quite interesting," Shanda said.

Silence filled the room. The rain could be heard outside the old mansion. Shane looked at Shanda. Her eyes met his.

"Shanda, I love you," he said, kissing her sweet lips.

Together their tongues merged. Shanda could feel the warmth of his body. Shane kissed under her chin and down her neck. Suddenly, another loud thunderous crash echoed through the forest. It startled them.

"Will you hold me, Shane?" she asked.

Shane put his arms around her and they both fell asleep.

A small ship departed from the planet Almonis Tarque. It was a world far from the Third Tiffan Siram Empire's territory. The pilot was very concerned about his mission. His people had been analyzing and piecing together information for his mission for well over one hundred years. At one point in history, his race reigned in the First Tiffan Siram Empire. It came to be known as the Era of the Thraxians. The House of Teserane was in power for two thousand two hundred and three years—from the year 11005 to the year 13208. It was the first and only time a non-human race was in power in the imperium. The average Thraxian lived approximately four hundred years. The majority of the Tiffan Siram Galaxy's people were human. The galaxy became tired of the Thraxians ruling from the Imperial Throne for such a long period of time. The Thraxians were forced to step down and a period of interregnum followed.

Auranaxis looked at his reflection in his cockpit observation window. He smiled at his dog in the rear compartment of the ship. Auranaxis's face was similar to that of humans. His skin color was neon blue with a whitish tone to it. A long, coarse organ protruded from the back of his head and trailed down his back. The organ increased his awareness of other beings around him. Many Thraxians found the organ useful, but others considered it a burden. He did not have any hair on top of his head, but in back, he had long, flowing, white hair. He was proud of his people's history. He thought the humans treated the Thraxians unfairly. But Auranaxis knew that the people who treated the Thraxians unfairly throughout history were evil people. He knew there were many good humans in existence too. The Third Tiffan Siram Empire sure did not have any of the good humans controlling it. His people were outraged by the actions of the Third Tiffan Siram Empire and the Universal Expanse Church. The Thraxians knew that it would not be long before the evil union of the government and the church would engulf the entire galaxy. That is why his mission was so important. It was a religious mission. He was willing to die to complete his tasks. He maneuvered the ship toward his destination and increased the ship's speed beyond that of light.

Sunlight shined through the bedroom window of the old mansion. Shane and Shanda awoke and yawned simultaneously.

"Man, it sure did feel good to get some sleep," Shane said.

"It sure did. Are you ready to hit the road?"

Shane sat up on the edge of the bed and rubbed his eyes. "Yeah, I'm ready."

They stood up and made their way back through the hallway. Passing the kitchen, they turned left and stepped onto a small back porch. Shane noticed a skeleton just outside the back door. As they stepped over the skeleton, Shanda made an awful face. She looked from the old bones on the ground to the cemetery across the trail.

"What's wrong?" Shane asked.

"I don't know. It just seems that life is so fragile. It passes by so quickly. We have to make the best of it by doing what's right."

Shane did not know what to say. He put his arm around her.

"Let's get out of here," she said.

Passing through the back yard of the old mansion, they headed for the trail. Soon, the sight of the graveyard was gone. It was replaced with many trees on either side of the trail.

"This trail should lead us toward Thisilia," Shane said.

Decorated in its aura of colors, the surrounding forest was breathtaking. The sound of birds could be heard chirping in the trees nearby. The shifting sound of stones under Shane's and Shanda's feet frightened several small animals along the edge of the trail. They scattered from the trail's edge and ran for shelter. Ahead of them, the space between the trees became wider. A soft padding of green grass carpeted the forest on either side of the trail. White flowers were spread throughout the green grass. The soft sound of flowing water could be heard in the distance. Shanda saw a small waterfall. The stream led through the forest toward the Slave Sea. After they had traveled a great distance, they noticed the town of Thisilia ahead of them.

"We're almost there," Shane said.

Soon, the forest ended to reveal the town. His spaceship could be seen in the distance.

As they approached the ship, Shane asked Shanda to wait by the ship while he went into the old building. He thanked Morrison for watching his ship while he was away. As Shane left the building, Morrison turned to face the two Third Tiffan Siram Empire Troops that stood hidden around a corner. The troops had arrived at the stable just minutes before Shane and had attached a device to his ship. Morrison did not want to betray Shane, but he had no choice. If he did not tell the troops the information they wanted to know about Shane, they would have killed him.

After they entered the ship, Shane started the engines. The ship slowly lifted from the surface of Myrath.

"Man, I sure am glad to be off that planet," Shanda said.

"Yeah, me too. Can you open the refrigerator back there and see if there is anything to eat?" he asked.

"Sure," Shanda said. "But first, let me tend to your shoulder with a med kit."

"There is a med kit in the back," he said.

They headed toward Toris at lightspeed.

CHAPTER NINE

THORTON PACED THE length of the sanctuary in deep thought. He felt very powerful with his new position. Nevertheless, he was concerned about the Third Tiffan Siram Empire. Was this unification between the government and the church a wise move? Thorton kept asking himself the question. Thorton's aide walked into the sanctuary, the sound of his entrance echoing high into the arches.

"Leenith, what brings you by this afternoon?" Thorton asked.

"Boris Anathor will be arriving here on Troth in about ten minutes. I was just informed," Leenith said.

Thorton's face turned white. "This comes as a surprise."

"Perhaps he *wanted* to make it a bit of a surprise, to catch you off guard."

"Do you know what this pertains to?" Thorton asked.

"Yes. It concerns the new religious laws that were put into effect."

"Oh. When he arrives, tell him I can be found in here," Thorton said.

"Okay," Leenith said. He exited the sanctuary and silence returned.

Thorton became very nervous. He continued to pace the floor.

Soon, the sanctuary door opened. A large man walked in. He wore a long beard. Thorton turned around to face him.

"Thorton, how are you?" Boris asked.

"Good. And you?"

"Fine. I've come to discuss the enforcement of the new religious laws with you. I hope I didn't catch you in the middle of something."

"No, you didn't. I was just thinking about the new laws myself."

"May I sit down?" Boris asked.

"Sure."

They both sat in the pews of the sanctuary.

"The new laws are working very well. Many people are coming to respect the new union of the Third Tiffan Siram Empire and the Universal Expanse Church. Those who continue to rebel against us will be killed. Thorton, I will not let the Third Tiffan Siram Empire be harassed by these outlaws. We are enforcing laws to help the people of this galaxy. They will soon come to realize that. My officials have established enforcement outposts throughout the Third Tiffan Siram Empire's jurisdiction. For those who continue to rebel, there is only death."

"I see," Thorton said.

"With your communications with the other churches on the outside, it will be possible to make the entire Tiffan Siram Galaxy a better place. Once we expand to the outside, our manifesto will be complete. The galaxy will be more pleasing in your God's eyes. Also, the profits we will receive after the expansion will be enormous. The galactic market will be much greater," Boris said.

"I contacted one of the other churches today. They expressed concern about the merge. They didn't give me a definite answer whether they would join us," Thorton said.

"Keep trying," Boris said as he stood from the pew.

"Yeah, I'll do that."

Shane could almost feel the cold temperature outside the ship. He maneuvered it through a snow storm in the northern region of Toris. Snow and ice slammed into the observation window. White was the only thing to be observed.

"It's a good thing the ship can be navigated by a computer. I sure couldn't do it myself in this terrible storm," Shane said, his face tightening.

Shanda cuddled up next to Shane at the controls. He noticed her beautiful eyes surveying his every move.

"You're sexy, Shane," she said.

He blushed. "Oh, Shanda, I love you," he said with a smile.

"So, is it gonna be cold where we're going?" she asked.

"From what I remember from studying The Lost Scroll in college, the Namaas Forest covers one third of the planet. It is located around the equator, so it should be warm," Shane said.

"That's good," Shanda said.

Eventually, the snow and ice dissipated. Sunshine emitted through the window of the ship. The view slowly changed from tundra and snow to a cold desert. Ripples of sand decorated each sand dune. Many old tree stumps could be seen, each with a smooth texture formed from the shifting sands. Both large and small stones were scattered throughout the desert in detail. Several immense outcrops protruded through the beige sands. As they flew closer toward their destination, the desert was left far behind. It had faded into a field of golden grass. The climate became warmer and many trees appeared. They flew over several small lakes.

"The scanners are picking up seven large objects. They must be the statues that the Scyllian Clan built. I'm *sure* they are. I'm also picking up a metal object," Shane said.

"Do you think that's where this treasure is?"

"Yes, I sure do. I didn't think it would be this easy to find. That's strange," Shane said, a look of wonder on his face.

"I wonder what the metal object is," Shanda said.

"It could be a small building or something like that. From what the computer is telling me, we are going to have to land the ship quite a few kilometers from our destination. The trees are too thick to land there. If we had a smaller ship, we might be able to. I know this ship is small, but not small enough for that. It looks like a road goes in that direction, however," Shane said.

They passed over several tall pine trees that seemed to reach up at them. Shane maneuvered the ship around and landed it in an open area where there were fewer trees. The front of the ship settled onto an ancient, paved road while the rear settled in the clearing. Shanda excitedly headed for the ship door.

"Shanda, wait!"

"What?"

"I have to check the planet's air pressure first. It might have changed from when this planet was populated."

He punched several keys on the computer keyboard, and the information rolled onto the screen.

"The sensors say it's fine. Go ahead," he said.

Shanda opened the ship door and stepped out onto the edge of the pavement. Shane transferred the coordinates to the AGT that was in the cargo hold. He grabbed a few bottles of water from the refrigerator and two laser rifles. He went down the metal steps and out the door.

"Can you hold on to these for a minute, Shanda? I have to get the anti-gravitational transport from the cargo hold," Shane said.

"Sure," she said, taking the water and rifles.

Shane opened the cargo hold doors at the side of the ship. He crawled into it and disconnected a wire harness from the AGT's outlet. After removing the AGT from its compartment, he shut the cargo hold doors.

"Hop in," Shane said.

Shanda stepped into the AGT. Shane made a few minor adjustments on the anti-gravitational unit beneath the transport. Then he joined Shanda and started the engine. With a hiss, the AGT lifted a meter from the ground.

"This thing is cool," she said with intrigue.

"Yeah, it will be a lot cooler once we get going," Shane said, wiping the perspiration from his brow.

"What is this I'm sitting on?" Shanda pulled a wrench out from underneath her.

"Oh, that's a wrench that I dropped down into the cargo hold earlier when I was bypassing the engine governor," Shane said.

He steered the AGT around toward the road and turned on the computer. A computer image of their destination was displayed on the screen. They headed down the road at a fast speed. The blowing winds shifted their hair around in all directions.

Countless trees grew on either side of the road. There were many different types of trees. The pine trees stood taller than the rest. Several small trees grew up through the pavement of the ancient road. Many of the wooded surroundings were decorated with a brilliant display of colors. Red and yellow leaves stood out brightly against the light green leaves and the dark green pines. The colorful forest's view slowly changed as many dead trees appeared. Soon, the majority of the trees were dead and rotted.

"That sign back there said that we're entering Sypron Swamp," Shane said.

"I know. I saw it. The swamp looks quite eerie, if you ask me," Shanda said, peering off into the swamp.

Numerous trees projected diagonally from the greenish-black waters. A network of connecting vines hung from the rotted trees. Many waterlogged trees were overlaid with a slippery, green moss. Deep in the swamp, the trees thinned rapidly. On either side of the road, the low-lying marsh's waters expanded as far as the eye could see. The stagnant waters seemed to begin flowing. Shane and Shanda gazed at the road before them. Ahead of them, the swamp suddenly dropped approximately thirty meters on each side of the road. The swamp waters descended over an edge and into a large river. An ancient concrete bridge crossed over the river. Green, opaque colored water rushed through the wide river below the bridge. As they crossed the bridge, they noticed the swamp draining over the bank into the river on the other side. The scene was similar to the riverbank behind them. Beyond the river, the low-lying swamp slowly faded away as the lush forest returned. The tall trees loomed above on high ridges on either side of the road. Shane and Shanda flew past what seemed to be an old restaurant on their left. There was a broken window in the front of the ancient restaurant. Old leaves and shrubbery decorated the front entrance.

"It's been at least one thousand two hundred years since this planet's been set aside as a memorial and all of its inhabitants evicted," Shane said.

"That long? With all the cracks and weeds in the road, you can tell it's been a long time with no upkeep," Shanda said.

To their left, they saw two whitish-gray wolves standing high on the ridge, their whitish-blue eyes scanning the forest. As the AGT flew by, they became frightened and fled into the woods. A few kilometers ahead of the AGT, Shane and Shanda saw what seemed to be another bridge. As they came closer, they discovered that it was another bridge. Unlike the first concrete bridge, this one was curved as the road turned to the left. This bridge crossed a canyon. The sheer cliffs dropped approximately five kilometers straight down. Shane stopped the AGT in the center of the bridge. They both peered over the edge from within the AGT. Far below, the trees of the forest resembled tiny dots. A layer of misty fog blanketed the tiny dots. Across the ravine there was a large waterfall. Its water dropped over the edge and fell far below to quench the thirst of the earth. They heard the roar of the rushing water as its continuous echo filled the canyon. The sun's rays emitted through the clouds and brightened the green foliage along the edge of the cliffs.

Shane looked at Shanda as she stared at the waterfall. She was so beautiful, her long, blond hair glistening in the sun. Shane managed to attract her attention from the falls.

"Shanda, I've been thinking about something for a long time now. I love you so much. I want to spend my life with you. Will you marry me?"

"Oh, Shane… Oh, Shane, I'd love to. I'd love to. I thought you'd never ask."

She smiled as tears started flowing down her face, like miniature waterfalls. Shane returned a smile as their lips met. Her fine lips felt warm against his. He hugged her tight.

"You'll make the best wife in the entire Tiffan Siram Galaxy," Shane said, returning to the controls of the AGT.

Shanda blushed. "I wouldn't want anyone else in the galaxy but you, Shane."

They continued across the bridge toward a series of ascending curves. To their right, there was a grayish-brown wall of rock that extended upward. On top of the rock wall, the tall pine trees reached toward the sky. To their left, many trees filled a shallow valley. Beyond the winding curves, the road reached the top of its ascension.

"According to the computer, those large objects that we scanned are about a kilometer off the road to our right. We're not going to be able to fly the AGT through the forest and rocky areas," Shane said.

He pulled off to the side of the road and parked the AGT beside a large rock. As its engines wound down, it slowly settled to the ground.

"I hope we can find it all right without the computer," Shanda said.

"Yeah, me too. It should be straight off to the right about a kilometer," Shane said, stepping out of the AGT.

Shanda set the laser rifles on the large rock next to the AGT and took a long drink of water. She passed the water bottle to Shane. After he satisfied his thirst, he slung one of the laser rifles over his shoulder. Shanda did the same.

"Ready?" he asked.

"After you," she said.

They headed into the mountainous forest.

A massive, armored ship settled onto the pavement next to the *Star Crystal,* its bluish surface shining from the sun. A hatch opened with a hiss, and a cloud of smoke drifted into the air. Two armed troops strode down a few metals stairs and onto the pavement. They wore special armored suits and helmets. Large laser cannons were held tight in their gloved hands. Many other special weapons were fixed to their belt gear. They scanned the forest and gazed down the road toward Sypron Swamp. Through the high definition visor connected to their armored helmets, the surrounding scenery became more enhanced and sharp. It enabled them to seek out and destroy the enemy much quicker. Three additional men exited the armored ship. They were dressed in light gray uniforms with black boots. Two of them quickly withdrew an anti-gravitational transport from the ship's cargo hold. The other uniformed man retrieved the homing beacon from Shane's ship. It was attached to the ship while it was parked at the stable in Thisilia back on Myrath. The two armored troops stepped into the AGT and engaged its engines. It rose from the pavement. They headed toward Sypron Swamp. The three uniformed men returned to the ship. The ship's pilot and navigator monitored the AGT and set their communicators on standby.

As Shane and Shanda stepped over a rock hill, they noticed a clearing ahead of them. They walked through the narrow opening and stopped in their tracks. They gazed at the scene ahead of them. Seven colossal statues of angels stood before them. The towering stone figures seemed to stare down at them. Their wings extended high into the trees. Three of them stood to the left, three of them stood to the right, and one stood in the center. Behind the angels there was a smooth rock wall. Vegetation grew all around the mountain wall. Directly behind the center angel, there was an opening to a cavern. The entrance to the cavern was smoothly engraved with elaborate designs.

"This is it! The Ojenis Temples, we've found them!" Shane said with excitement.

Shanda said nothing as she continued to stare in awe at the

towering angels.

"Shanda, come on," Shane said as he walked toward the cavern entrance.

She followed Shane into the Ojenis Temples.

"This is amazing, Shane."

"I know."

"The Scyllian Clan must have really worked hard to construct these temples," Shanda said.

"Yeah, whatever it was they found must be worth something. They wouldn't undergo the construction of these temples if it wasn't. We should be careful to avoid any traps, just in case the Scyllian Clan set any," Shane said.

They continued into the cavern, walking up a set of stone steps. Shanda saw something over the top step. When they reached the top of the stairs, they discovered what Shanda had seen. A large fountain was located in the center of a chamber. Its water spewed high into the arches of the chamber and came crashing down in a continuous splash.

"It's beautiful," Shanda said as she observed the flowing waters.

Shane walked around the right side of the fountain. Shanda proceeded around the left. As she strode past the fountain, a misty spray of refreshing water settled upon her. Three portals were located on the far side of the fountain. One was located straight ahead of them, one diagonally to the left, and one diagonally to the right. Each of the portals had tall stone pillars on either side of them. The stone pillars revealed a greenish tint. High above the chamber floor, large slabs of stone connected each set of pillars. The stone slabs were engraved with a multitude of tiny inscriptions. Shanda followed Shane through the portal on the left. It led to a large room with designs of art on the smooth walls and ceiling. Nothing else was in the room. Looking in the room through the portal on the right, they discovered the same thing—another empty room with designs on the walls and ceiling. They returned to the fountain chamber and walked through the center portal. It led to another set of stone steps. As they traveled up the stairs, the echo of their steps rang out through the temples. The steps ended at another immense chamber. It was dark inside; however, there was enough light to see. What they saw astonished them. They looked forward with sudden wonder. Seven gold chests were displayed before them. Like the towering angel statues outside the cavern, the chests were fixed in the same position. At the far end of the chamber, three were located on the left, three were located on the right, and one in the center. Shane walked over to one of the gold chests and opened its heavy lid. His eyes became wide with surprise. The chest was filled with gold, silver, and a variety of jewels. He opened another chest and saw the same thing.

"I can't believe this! Why would the Third Tiffan Siram Empire want to kill me over this. I mean, I know it's worth countless credits, but this can't be the treasure that I messed up my life for. It just can't be! Shanda, what am I going to do?" Shane's face was covered with disappointment.

"Don't worry, Shane. You didn't know. Perhaps it's best that things turned out this way. At least we can be together," Shanda said as she put her arms around him.

"You are my real treasure, Shanda," he said, smiling.

"Those treasure chests are not the actual treasure that the Third Tiffan Siram Empire is searching for," a voice behind them said.

Shane and Shanda quickly turned around with their laser rifles drawn.

"There is no need for those; I mean you no harm. My name is Auranaxis," he said as he walked from the shadows of the chamber.

The tall alien looked strange in the darkened chamber. He held out his hand to Shane. Shane lowered his weapon and shook the rough, bluish hand.

"A Thraxian…" That is all that Shane could manage.

"Yes. I sensed your presence as you entered the temples. My name is Auranaxis," he repeated.

"I'm Shane Aslat and this is my fiancée, Shanda Rubine."

"I am very delighted to meet you both," Auranaxis said.

"You mentioned that you sensed us coming. How?" Shanda asked.

"We Thraxians have special organs in the back of our heads. It enables us to expand our awareness of other beings around us," he explained.

"I see," Shanda said, looking at the organ in the back of his head.

"You said that this is not the treasure that the Third Tiffan Siram Empire is looking for. How do you know?" Shane asked.

"Well, they probably wouldn't mind having these chests also, but the real treasure is in there," Auranaxis said, pointing toward a doorway in the shadows.

"What is it?" Shanda asked.

"I don't know. I was in there inspecting it when I sensed you two coming. So, I came out here and hid in the shadows."

"How did you know that it existed?" Shane asked.

"My people have been studying this treasure for centuries. That is why the Thraxians ruled in the First Tiffan Siram Empire. It was an easy access to information and files. We've been piecing together relics from the Scyllian Clan for centuries. The Lost Scroll was not the only piece of evidence left behind that explains this treasure's existence. There are numerous others—less significant—that helped locate the Ojenis Temples. Back when my people ruled the empire, this planet had not yet been set aside as a memorial and forgotten. We didn't make the connection at the time we were in power. Us Thraxians live much longer than you humans. For over one hundred years, I've personally prepared for this mission. I am on a mission from my government to come here and retrieve the last remnant of the Scyllian Clan. It is a very crucial remnant. From our studies, we have discovered that this treasure is of a religious significance," Auranaxis said.

"I don't know too much about Thraxians. I've only seen a couple in my life. What is your government's part in all this?" Shane asked.

"The Thraxian Government has built up tremendous armed forces over the years. We have anticipated that the Third Tiffan Siram Empire would attempt to conquer the entire galaxy. The Universal Expanse Church is making things very difficult for the people of this galaxy also. My government knows that this treasure is of vital importance. That is why I have been sent here to Toris. When I return to Almonis Tarque, we will launch a full scale assault against the Third Tiffan Siram Empire and the Universal Expanse Church. This war will be on a galactic scale. We Thraxians have countless outposts across the galaxy where there are multitudes of spaceports. Each spaceport has at least eight hundred armored spaceships with powerful laser cannons and torpedoes. The Thraxian Government is working in cooperation with a church group. This group divided from the Universal Expanse Church when they merged with the Third Tiffan Siram Empire. Our church group will not be involved with the war effort; however, they will help those in need. I have a question for you, Shane," Auranaxis said.

"What?" he asked.

"How did you know about the Ojenis Temples?" Auranaxis asked.

"I came across The Lost Scroll at an art festival. The Third Tiffan Siram Empire found out I had it. I've kind of been on the run ever since," Shane said, showing Auranaxis the scroll from his pocket.

"My people knew that The Lost Scroll was roaming around the Tiffan Siram Galaxy somewhere. We've been searching for that for centuries too," Auranaxis said.

"Why are you telling us all this information? How do you know we are not from the Third Tiffan Siram Empire?" Shanda asked.

"I overheard you talking when you discovered the treasure chests. You mentioned that the Third Tiffan Siram Empire was trying to kill you. So, I knew you weren't from the Third Tiffan Siram Empire," Auranaxis said.

"My ship's computer did not scan any ships in the area. How did you get— Oh, that's right. We did pick up a metal object near these temples. Our ship could not land here. Your ship must be pretty small," Shane said.

"Yes, it is a small fighter ship. Well, shall we see the treasure in the next chamber?" Auranaxis gestured toward the door in the shadows.

They walked into the next chamber. This chamber was small and darker yet. A stone table extended out from the far wall. On the table was a small stone container. A stone cross was hung on the wall above the table.

"This is it," Auranaxis said.

"What is it?" Shanda asked.

"I don't know. I couldn't seem to get it open. It has a seemingly unremovable lid. I don't want to smash it because it might have something breakable inside," Auranaxis said.

"I wonder why the Scyllian Clan did not set any traps to protect this," Shane said.

"From what we've studied about the Scyllian Clan, they did not want to hurt anyone. They just wanted to preserve this treasure that they had found here in the Namaas Forest," Auranaxis said.

Shanda picked up the stone container and observed it. She tried to remove the cover. It would not budge.

"I can pry it open with this dagger I have attached to my boot that I got from the Tulli Castle," Shane said.

She handed it to Shane. His grip slipped and the stone container fell to the floor, smashing into many fragments. Among those fragments lay the treasure.

"The Holy Bible." Shane read the title.

Auranaxis picked the book up from the dusty floor and examined it. He thumbed through it.

"I suspected such," he said, handing the book to Shane.

Shane opened the book and searched through it.

"It seems to be God's Written Word for mankind. It's like an instruction manual for our lives. Oh, do I ever want to read this," Shane said.

"Millennia ago, people of the galaxy did not think of it as a treasure. As a result, the Written Word of God faded away over the years. This is most likely the last copy in the entire galaxy," Auranaxis said.

"We have to take this to a printing company," Shanda said.

"Yes. We can do that on Almonis Tarque. We have a very large printing house there. You two—" Auranaxis stopped talking.

"What is it?" Shanda asked.

"Shhh. I sense two people coming. Did you two come alone?"

"Yes," Shane said.

"Let's go back out into the other chamber and hide in the shadows. It worked before," Auranaxis said.

They returned to the chamber containing the seven gold chests of treasure. As they squatted in the shadows, two armored troops entered the chamber. Laser cannons swung left and right as they advanced farther into the chamber. One of them turned around and looked into the shadows with his high definition visor. As he turned around with the laser cannon, a large dog came from the stairs, running with great speed. He jumped high and knocked one of the Third Tiffan Siram Empire Troops over. It gave Shane and Shanda enough time to fire their laser rifles. Intense blue beams sliced through the darkness of the chamber. Before dying, one of the troopers managed to fire off one shot of his laser cannon. The beam of destructive light hummed by the three of them and penetrated the wall. A shower of stone particles flew into Shanda's face. She screamed. The scream echoed throughout the Ojenis Temples.

"Shanda! Are you all right?" Shane asked, putting his arm around her.

"I think so. It burns," she said.

Shane looked at the speckled cheek. He brushed some loose stone particles onto the floor.

"It doesn't look that bad. It will probably hurt for a while, though," he said.

"Nice job, Teraster. Come here, boy," Auranaxis called his dog.

The dog pranced over to his master.

"Thank God for miracles," Shanda said, wincing from the pain.

"Yeah. He's a good dog. Aren't ya, boy?" he said, petting the dog.

The two Third Tiffan Siram Empire Troops lay dead on the chamber floor. The three of them stood up from their squatting positions. Suddenly a beeper started sounding on Auranaxis's belt.

"That can't be! They were going to wait for my return with the treasure. Something must've gone wrong," Auranaxis said.

"What are you talking about?" Shanda asked.

"That beeper meant that the assault has begun. The Tiffan Siram Galactic War has officially begun. For some reason, they are attacking early. Something must be wrong. I have to get back to Almonis Tarque. Are you two coming with me?" he asked.

"Yes. We are all in this together," Shane said.

They left the Ojenis Temples and stopped near the angel statues.

"They must have followed us here from Myrath. But how? How did they know I was on Myrath? Oh…"

"What?" Shanda asked.

"They must have figured that I would go to Myrath because of the permits that I requested to come and see you."

"Those two troops must have come in a military ship. If they followed you, they probably landed by your ship. You said that you couldn't land near the temples because your ship was too large. If it is that far from here to your ship, why don't you return to it? By the time you get there, I will have destroyed their ship," Auranaxis suggested.

"Sounds like a plan," Shane said.

Auranaxis and his dog, Teraster, departed and headed for his fighter ship. Shane and Shanda left the sacred place and proceeded toward the AGT.

Without warning, Auranaxis attacked the Third Tiffan Siram Empire's armored ship. An explosion followed the attack. A large ball of fire rolled into the blue sky. Shane and Shanda saw the black smoke from the road. When they reached their ship, they came to a stop. The flames from the Third Tiffan Siram Empire ship's shell died down. Auranaxis landed his ship on the road and stepped out.

"Is your ship all right?" he asked.

Shane walked over to the side of the ship. Scorch marks and black deposits covered the side of the ship.

"She looks like she's been in battle," Shane said, laughing. "It will be fine."

"Here's the Holy Bible," Shanda said, handing it to Auranaxis.

"Oh, thank you, Shanda," he said, receiving the book from her.

She could see that he was very concerned about this sudden war starting.

"We'll follow you. Give us your coordinates over the communicator once we're in the ship," Shane said.

"Okay," Auranaxis said.

Shane quickly returned the AGT to the cargo hold and sealed the compartment. They went aboard the *Star Crystal* and started its engines. Auranaxis gave the coordinates of Almonis Tarque to Shane over the communicator. Both ships lifted from the surface of the desolate planet.

Chapter Ten

On Almonis Tarque, the seat of the Thraxian Government was located in a place called Lysith Palace. The palace was surrounded by the great city of Shenix Falls. Lysith Palace was an enormous structure with many towers and spires extending into the sky. High above the ground, a large landing platform extended out from one of the palace towers. Several ships were parked on the platform.

Auranaxis, Shane, and Shanda had just arrived. As they followed Auranaxis along the corridors of the Lysith Palace, Shane and Shanda surveyed the palace walls. Many paintings decorated the corridors. Someone with a great talent designed each picture with an intricate scene. There were many nature and space scenes. Large pillars stood at each corridor intersection. They soon came to a large door. Auranaxis opened it and they walked inside.

"If you will wait here, I will find someone who can accommodate you with your own quarters. It should only be a few minutes before someone can assist you. I will see you soon. I have to report to the government administrator with the treasure and find out why the war has begun so soon. Make yourselves comfortable. I'll see you later,"

Auranaxis said as he left the room.

Shanda watched him leave, his long, white hair flowing behind him. "He tries to be so nice."

"Yes. The Thraxian people have a sense of peace and compassion to them," Shane said as he made himself comfortable on a couch.

The room contained a beautiful model of the Lysith Palace in the center of it. Two white leather couches sat along one wall. A drinking fountain was directly across from the entrance.

"I wonder what's going on. Do you think the war has really begun?" Shanda asked.

"I don't know if it has, but when it does, there are going to be battles all across the galaxy. It's not—"

Shane paused as the door opened. A Thraxian person stepped into the room.

"Hello. My name is Tharakon. I'll be showing you where your quarters are," he said.

"All right," Shane said, standing from the couch. "So, do you know what's going on with the war?"

"Yes. The Third Tiffan Siram Empire and the Universal Expanse Church began executing its people for not obeying their new laws. We could not stand by and let that continue without launching the war when we did. It couldn't wait until Auranaxis's return. The original plan included Auranaxis as a strategic relief support for the initial strike teams that departed from Almonis Tarque. Unfortunately, we had to use someone else," Tharakon said.

"Where is Auranaxis now?" Shanda asked.

"The government administrator has sent him out alone as a secondary strategic relief support for those troops from Almonis Tarque. The other Thraxian warriors throughout the galaxy have their own relief support," Tharakon said.

They followed Tharakon down another series of corridors.

"Would you like separate quarters?" he asked.

"No, thank you. One will be fine," Shane said as he put his arm around Shanda.

After turning a corner, Tharakon came to a halt. "Here it is. If there is anything that you need, please let someone know by using the intercom inside the room."

"Okay. Thanks a lot," Shane said.

"You are most welcome," he said.

As Tharakon left, they entered into their quarters. It was a fairly large dwelling with a kitchen, bathroom, bedroom, and living room.

"I'm going to hit the shower. See if you can get someone over the intercom. Ask them if we can get some clean clothes," Shane said.

"Yeah. Don't be too long. I need to take one too," she said.

Shane disappeared into the bathroom.

Auranaxis flew toward the planet Amveries to help relieve some of the Thraxian warriors there. It had been reported that the Third Tiffan Siram Empire Troops were thick and fierce at the planet's main outpost. The Thraxians needed as much help as possible. It was an intense battle. As his fighter ship cut through the thick clouds of Amveries, he thought of the fleet of Thraxians that had flown onward toward the battle near the planet Delbis Salias. They were also going to need much help. Auranaxis said a prayer for them.

His computer screen displayed two enemy ships approaching from the starboard side. He cut his engine's speed and swerved around behind them. Firing his lasers, he destroyed one of the two ships. It exploded into a ball of fire. The remaining ship tried to escape, but Auranaxis quickly caught up and fired his lasers. The ship erupted in a violent explosion. With a sigh of relief, Auranaxis proceeded toward his destination.

Soon, the thickness of the clouds dissipated and a fiery battle could be seen below. Auranaxis landed his ship in a secluded area and gathered his supplies. He put on a pair of glasses to protect his eyes from the intense laser fire. Grabbing his laser rifle, he headed toward the battle. His people needed an extra warrior.

"Auranaxis, I sure am glad to see you," one of the men said, crouching behind a shelled-out fighter ship.

"I heard you guys needed some help out here," Auranaxis said.

Suddenly, intense laser fire was streaking through the air. Several beams struck the damaged fighter ship, sending a shower of sparks overhead.

"We've been trying to hold them off for days now. We don't seem to be effective. There are too many of them. Do you have any ideas?" one of the men asked.

"Well, Commander Nottoran, I do have an idea. That's why I came down here. I have a small missile aboard my ship. I'm here to warn you before I drop it. The entire front line is going to have to retreat back about three kilometers. Is there any other Third Tiffan Siram Empire Troops on the planet besides the ones here?" Auranaxis asked.

"There is one more regiment in the southern hemisphere. They are supposedly holding the people of a town prisoner for not obeying their laws. I think they will be much easier to take than these troops. They've been here for days. They are dug in pretty well," Nottoran said.

"Well, the missile should take care of these troops. Why don't you guys retreat to your ships and head down to the southern hemisphere?" Auranaxis suggested.

"I think that will work. Thanks for your help, Auranaxis," Nottoran said.

"No problem."

"So, what are you going to do after this?" Nottoran asked.

"The Thraxian administrator sent me out to relieve our people at key battle sites. I've been out here for several days now. There is a battle raging in the Ythorn Asteroid Mass. There are many asteroid miners trapped inside one of the main asteroids. I'm going to see if I can help," Auranaxis said.

"Good luck."

"Yeah, you too."

"Okay, let's head out. Get back to the ships. We're going to the southern hemisphere to attack the regiment there," Commander Nottoran told his troops.

As they retreated to their ships, Auranaxis returned to his. When the last of the Thraxian ships lifted from the surface, Auranaxis flew his ship over the enemy and fired the missile. With an enormous vibration, the ground shook. Fire quickly engulfed the site and spread across the land. The cloud of fire extended upward toward the sky. As Auranaxis's ship ascended higher into the atmosphere, the intense flash ripped through the sky. He shielded his eyes to protect them from the blinding light. Soon, he was back in the darkness of space. He set a course for the Ythorn Asteroid Mass.

Shane and Shanda had just finished eating a lavish dinner when there was a signal at their quarters door. Shane opened it.

"Oh, Tharakon. What can I do for you?" Shane asked.

"Desinarr, the Thraxian Government administrator, wants to see you," Tharakon said.

"Okay. If you'll wait a second I'll let Shanda know that I'm going," Shane said.

Shane informed Shanda that he was leaving to see the administrator. He followed Tharakon through the Lysith Palace to Desinarr's office. Tharakon opened the door and they stepped inside.

"Hello. You must be Shane Aslat. My name is Desinarr. I am the Thraxian Government administrator. Welcome to the Lysith Palace. I hope your stay here will be an enjoyable one."

"Thank you," Shane said.

"Have a seat, Shane, Tharakon." He gestured to the two chairs in front of his desk.

They both sat down and looked at Desinarr. Shane could see an anxiety in the alien's eyes.

"I had Tharakon bring you here for several reasons. One of them is this," he said, pointing to the Holy Bible on his desk. "This book is the Word of God. My people have been looking for this treasure for centuries upon centuries. The Third Tiffan Siram Empire has been searching for it in recent years. They learned about The Lost Scroll some time ago. I understand that you managed to find the scroll. That is how you found the treasure. It's a coincidence that Auranaxis and you met there at the same time. In fact, it's a miracle. Shane, I would like to know if you want to help the Thraxian people in this war. We can really use your help."

"I would be glad to help out. And I can confidently speak for Shanda when I say that. I am totally against what the Third Tiffan Siram Empire and the Universal Expanse Church are doing," Shane said.

"It means a great deal to us. I would also like to know if you still want to keep The Lost Scroll. If not, it would be most appreciated if you would let us add it to our collection of other historical evidence that the Scyllian Clan left behind," Desinarr said.

"Sure, you can have it. I have no need for it any longer," Shane said.

"What I would like you to do, first of all, is to bring the Holy Bible to one of our local churches here in Shenix Falls. This church is not connected with the Universal Expanse Church. It is a *real* church. I would like you and the pastor to read through this Bible. It might take a few months, but it will be well worth it. I believe there is a treasure within this treasure. And to find the Truth of God, one has to search the Scriptures carefully. It can easily be interpreted the wrong way. We must make sure that it is understood well. When you've completed the book, I want you to bring it to the government's printing house and have five trillion copies made. Also, have it translated to digital files that can be distributed. The galaxy can't afford to lose the Word of God again. It might take a couple of months for that, but when the printed Bibles and digital files are finished, bring them back to the church. The pastor will see that they are distributed throughout the galaxy. Pastor Renlin is expecting you."

"I'll do my best. Also, if you need any assistance with anything pertaining to the electronics area, I am quite skilled," Shane said.

"Okay, I'll keep that in mind. Tharakon, could you please assist Shane on his mission?"

"Yes."

Shane and Tharakon stood from the chairs.

"Thank you so much for your help, Shane."

"You're welcome," he said.

They left Desinarr's office. The corridor was strangely quiet.

"I should tell Shanda that I will be leaving the palace for a while," Shane said.

"That would be fine," Tharakon said.

Explosions shook the temples of the Universal Expanse Church on Troth. Endless waves of fighter ships attacked the temples and the surrounding area. They destroyed the execution device in the rear of the temples. It had been used to slaughter the innocent people who did not obey the government and church's unjust laws.

Thorton and Leenith felt the heat waves of the massive explosions. They took shelter in a nearby shed. Thorton peered out the shed door and watched the temples slowly become rubble. As the high priest of the Universal Expanse Church, Thorton felt that he should do something about this attack. But he knew that he was not powerful. It seemed to him that the UEC was being paid back for some great sin.

"Do you hear that?" Leenith asked.

"Hear what?"

"There is a noise."

Suddenly, a missile struck near the shed. The flames consumed them. Gnashing their teeth from the pain, they fell to the floor. In seconds, their bodies were incinerated.

Shanda had been working on her wedding preparations for several months. Two female Thraxians were assisting her. She had such a beautiful wedding planned. She had not seen much of Shane. He was busy with the Bible printing. He even brought a copy to their quarters. She read the entire Old Testament and was looking forward to reading the New Testament. The book revealed God's love for his people. She was proud to be one of those people. She also wanted to help other people become Christians. She wanted to proclaim the good news of Jesus to anyone that would listen.

She continued designing her wedding bows. The two Thraxian assistants were in her quarters helping her.

"What do you think, Ameriss?" Shanda asked, holding up one of the bows.

"It's beautiful, Shanda."

"Maybe you should trim the edges a little more," the other assistant, Tereen, said.

"Yeah, maybe you're right. It does look a little wide. Do you really think that the wedding colors will be okay?" Shanda asked.

"Blue, beige, and mauve are beautiful colors for your wedding," Ameriss said.

"How much baby's breath do you want in the bride's maids' bouquets?" Tereen asked.

Shanda looked at the bouquet in Tereen's hand. "That's fine. Oh, I'm getting so excited. I can't wait to pick out my dress. I am so thankful that the Thraxian Government is paying for this wedding. It wouldn't be as elaborate if Shane and I did it on our own."

"So, who else is going to be in your wedding?" Tereen asked.

"Outside of you two, I'm not sure. I have to talk it over with Shane," Shanda said.

At that moment, Shane walked through the door. The three women looked up to see who it was.

"Hi, sweetheart. How are you doing?" Shanda asked.

"Good. I've been transporting Bibles from the printing house to the church all day. I'm tired. How's the wedding preparations going?" he asked.

"Great. How do you like the bows?"

"They're a little wide. Maybe you should trim the edges a little. What do you think?"

The women started laughing.

"What's so funny?" he asked. "Never mind. Don't tell me. I don't want to know."

He left the living room with a smile. In the kitchen, he grabbed a cold beverage from the refrigerator. Opening the bottle, he felt its condensation moisten his hand. He took a long drink and sighed. Shanda called him from the living room.

"Yeah?" he asked.

"There's someone at the door. Can you get it? We're busy."

"Sure," he said, walking to the door with the beverage in his hand.

It was Tharakon. He had a grim expression on his face.

"Something major has happened in the Tiffan Siram Galactic War. Desinarr wants to hold a meeting in the conference room immediately," Tharakon said.

"Do you know what it pertains to?" Shane asked.

"Something about the Third Tiffan Siram Empire destroying some type of system. I don't know the details. But he said that it's a galactic emergency," Tharakon said.

Shane's heart skipped a beat. He looked over at Shanda who heard the conversation.

"I'll be back as soon as possible," he told her.

He followed Tharakon to the conference room. Many key members of the Thraxian Government sat at a long table. Desinarr sat at the head of the table. Although Shane felt special to be invited to this meeting, he felt out of place. He and Tharakon sat down in the two empty chairs. Everyone's attention was focused on Desinarr. As Desinarr stood, the room became quiet.

"As some of you may already know, there has been a galactic emergency. This emergency pertains to the people under the Third Tiffan Siram Empire and the Universal Expanse Church's jurisdictions. We are not only fighting this war to maintain our own freedom, but we are also fighting this war to set the people under the Third Tiffan Siram Empire's jurisdiction free. What has happened is the Third Tiffan Siram Empire has destroyed their own digital currency computer system. Now, no one under their jurisdiction has the power to buy or sell. They have no way to eat or get things they need. All of their credits are destroyed. Also, the Third Tiffan Siram Empire has told the media that we destroyed the computer system. Now, the suffering people under the Third Tiffan Siram Empire are against us. Quite a plan that the Third Tiffan Siram Empire's come up with. However, there is good news. The Devrakian species has joined our fight. This is their representative, Calazen. He has a few words to say," Desinarr said, sitting back into his chair.

Shane's eyes were fixed on the new alien. He was a short creature with gray skin and large red eyes. A series of small ripples covered his bald head. He cleared his throat.

"The Devrakian people have always been against the Third Tiffan Siram Empire. My people were afraid of the Third Tiffan Siram Empire. We recently realized that something must be done to stop them. They want everything in the Tiffan Siram Galaxy to be united. They want one system for everything. According to them, small governments, small businesses, small churches, and small economies are breaking down and weakening the galaxy. They see the strength of a one galaxy government. What they fail to see is the people's will for freedom. Under the First and Second Tiffan Siram Empires, the people of the galaxy were free. But this Third Tiffan Siram Empire has to be destroyed. Now, my people feel the courage to join the Thraxian Government in the Tiffan Siram Galactic War. Thank you for accepting us," Calazen said with a reverberating voice.

He sat down and Desinarr rose once again.

"Not only have the Devrakian people joined in the war, many humans have joined as well. One of them is here. Shane Aslat, would you stand for a moment?" Desinarr said.

Shane stood for the government officials and then sat back down.

"This war is going to be a long, rough one. But with all of our forces across the galaxy, we have a very good chance of winning. We have to win, because if we lose, the evil Third Tiffan Siram Empire will engulf the entire galaxy. Let us pray, shall we?

"Dear God in heaven, You are our hope. You are our courage. We have fallen so short of Your expectations, yet You continue to have patience with us. Please forgive us for our sins, Lord. Please guide us with Your hand. Please fill us with Your Spirit. Thank you, Lord, for all the blessings you have given us. Please continue to bless us. We ask that You help us in this mighty war that has erupted across the galaxy. Please help us defeat our enemies. Please help us restore Your Divine Word throughout the galaxy once again. Thank You, Lord, for sending

Your son, Jesus, long ago so that we have a chance to live eternally with You. And thank You for the privilege of prayer. What would we do if we could not communicate with our Father? In Jesus's precious name, amen."

They all lifted their heads and looked back at Desinarr.

"This meeting is complete. You are dismissed," Desinarr said.

The people stood up from their chairs and slowly left the room.

"Shane, could I see you for a moment?" Desinarr asked.

Shane walked over to the head of the conference table. "What is it?"

"I have another mission for you. This one is much more involved with the war. Auranaxis has requested help out in the Ythorn Asteroid Mass. They need someone with electronics expertise. I told him that I would send you," Desinarr said.

"I don't have a fighter ship. And I don't know how to fly a Thraxian ship," Shane said.

"Oh, it's simple. I'll have Tharakon instruct you. It can't be any more difficult than your own ship."

"Okay," Shane said.

"Let me give you the details of the situation. A major battle has taken place in the Ythorn Asteroid Mass. We are winning the battle; however, one of the asteroids is a mining asteroid. There are many people trapped inside. Auranaxis is trying to help them. He needs some assistance. Here is a memory drive with the coordinates," Desinarr said, handing Shane the digital device.

"All right. I'll find Tharakon and have him teach me how to fly one of the Thraxian fighter ships," Shane said.

"Good luck," Desinarr said, patting Shane on the back.

"Thanks, I think," he said with a smile.

What did I get myself into? Shane asked himself as he left the conference room.

A massive space vessel was located near the Ythorn Asteroid Mass. It was one of the many Third Tiffan Siram Empire battleships in the galaxy. There were many docking bays, ports, and other structures protruding from the rigid surface of the ship. The ship seemed to be cold and desolate, yet it was swarming with activity. Countless fighter ships flew to and from the giant vessel.

Deep within the metal structure, an evil man plotted against the

Thraxian forces.

"While our fighter ships are keeping the Thraxian forces busy, we will fly the *Abbitarr* toward the mining asteroid. I want to finish it off. All of the Thraxians inside *will* die," Captain Ertlees of the *Abbitarr* said.

His lead officer sat across from him. They were in his private conference chamber.

"With another attack, we should be able to ignite the gas that is mined there. It's too bad we don't know where the location of the Thraxian Government is," the lead officer said.

"Time… In time, we will know. And when we find it, there will be hell to pay," Ertlees said with wide eyes.

"The way Emperor Boris Anathor spoke to the fleet earlier, he wants the Thraxian Government found soon. He didn't seem too pleased with our progress," Both said.

"Sometimes Boris thinks he knows everything. He wants everything done his way. Well, Both, if I am out here fighting, I am going to run the show my own way," Ertlees said, switching on the intercom. "This is Captain Ertlees. Maneuver the *Abbitarr* around toward the mining asteroid. Start cluster bombing the surface again. I want maximum power from the laser cannons too. This time, we're going to destroy that rock!"

"But if we get that close—"

"Just do what you're told!"

In the distance, Shane could see the asteroid mass. There were several asteroids the size of a small satellite. It was difficult to see through all the cosmic dust in the area. Shane scarcely saw the fighter ships attacking each other. From the great distance, their tiny lasers looked like small sparks. As he flew closer, Shane noticed the large battleship. It was moving upon a large asteroid. Small bombs dropped from its belly and penetrated the surface of the asteroid. Suddenly, lasers cut through the darkness of space and struck the asteroid. Shane then realized that it was the mining asteroid that was being attacked.

It's a good thing the fleet from Delbis Salias is on their way to assist in this battle, Shane thought.

Without warning, the mining asteroid exploded. The *Abbitarr* was pushed back from the force of the rocks. The massive battleship slammed against another large asteroid and, itself, exploded. The silent explosion quickly faded as the twisted metal fragments were sucked into the great vacuum of space. The mining asteroid continued to burst. It sent millions of tiny asteroids hurtling outward in every direction. The majority of the fighter ships battling in the area were instantly destroyed.

"Auranaxis! No!" Shane shouted.

Before Shane could think, asteroids from the explosion started plunging into his fighter ship. He quickly transferred all power to the front defense shields. The shields could not withstand the constant force of the asteroids. One by one, he lost power to the shields. He was headed straight for a large one. Shane managed to maneuver around it. The brown, icy rock drifted by, just centimeters from his ship. Abruptly, his ship's observation window cracked. It was a small crack, but his cockpit started losing pressure. A warning light started flashing on the control panel. Shane's mind raced for a solution. He found none.

As the air became thin, memories from the past started flashing through his mind. He saw Shanda with her beautiful smile and her long, blond hair. Oh, did he love her so. Then he saw himself as a young boy. His mother was looking down at him.

"Don't be too long. Dinner will be ready soon," she had said.

"I won't, Mom," he had said as he ran off to play.

He remembered going fishing on Elbi with his father and brother.

"Dad, Dad, I caught one!"

"Well, look at that. He's a pretty big one too."

Shanda flashed back into the picture.

"Oh, Shane, I'd love to. I thought you'd never ask."

Her words echoed through his mind. He thought about the treasure they had found. The Holy Bible… He thought about Jesus's love for His people.

Oh, dear Jesus, please help me! he cried.

A single tear rolled down his right cheek as his consciousness faded.

Shanda's cries echoed through the halls of the Lysith Palace. She had just received the news about Shane's accident. She ran through the corridors toward Desinarr's office. As she rounded a corner, she collided with Desinarr. They both fell to the palace floor.

"Oh, Shanda, are you okay?" he asked.

"Desinarr, what happened to Shane? Tharakon told me he's been in an accident," she said as she picked herself up from the floor.

As Desinarr stood, he saw the tears run down her face. "I was just on my way to see you. Yes, Shane's been in an accident. It is a good thing the fleet from Delbis Salias found him. Otherwise he would still be out there, dying."

"He's okay?" she asked with an expression of last hope.

"I don't know what kind of shape he's in, but he is still alive. He's at the Shenix Falls Medical Facility. Pastor Renlin is with him right now. I have to take care of a few important war matters, and then I will be going down there myself," Desinarr said.

"Is he the only one hurt?" she asked.

"No…well, yeah. The rest are dead. Auranaxis and the miners are dead. The squadron of fighter pilots are dead. It wasn't Shane's time to go," Desinarr said.

"Auranaxis…" She inhaled a deep breath. "I'm going to see Shane."

"I'll see you there shortly," he said.

Shanda headed for the ground level of the palace. The Shenix Falls Medical Facility was not far from the Lysith Palace. When she reached the palace parking lot, she got into her AGT.

As she quickly drove along the streets of Shenix Falls, she noticed the bright blue sky. She hoped that she would have something bright to look forward to when she reached the medical facility. Thoughts of Shane constantly crossed through her mind. She began quivering and pulled the AGT off to one side of the street. She lay her head on the steering control. When she regained control of her emotions, she continued onward. The only man she ever loved lay helpless in a hospital. What would she do without him? She could not bear the thought.

When she arrived at the medical facility, she parked her AGT and ran toward the door. The woman at the information desk saw her coming.

"Where's Shane? Shane Aslat?" she asked.

The woman checked the computer. "Second floor, room 202."

"Thanks," Shanda said, rushing toward the elevator.

When she reached the second level, she saw Pastor Renlin standing outside of room 202. He saw her approach from the elevator.

"Shanda."

"Is he okay?" she asked.

"He is doing much better. Just as the fleet from Delbis Salias tractor-beamed his ship aboard theirs, his ship's observation window shattered. He has cuts from some of the loose items that were in his cockpit. One of the items that cut him was a necklace. They tractor-beamed him aboard just in time," Renlin said.

"I want to see him," she said, walking toward his room.

Shane lay there in the bed, his eyes focused on the approaching figure. Several tubes were connected to him from nearby instruments. A bandage covered the left side of his jaw. He looked very pale.

"Hi, sweetheart," he managed.

"Shane, are you all right?" She reached out to hold his hand.

"I've felt better," he said softly.

"Oh, Shane, I'm so thankful that you're alive. I don't know what I'd do without you," she said as her tears returned.

Somehow, Shane found the strength to squeeze her hand tighter. He started crying. As his emotions overwhelmed him, the instrument next to his bed started beeping. A nurse quickly ran into the room to see what the problem was. When Shane calmed down, the nurse left the room.

"Did you hear about Auranaxis?" Shane asked.

"Yes. That is so tragic. He was such a nice person," Shanda said.

"The Third Tiffan Siram Empire killed him…along with the rest of the gas miners. But they were too close. The explosion destroyed their ship too," Shane said.

"It's a good thing the fleet that came from Delbis Salias found you," Shanda said.

"They came there to help fight a battle, and they end up saving my life." He shook his head.

"I hope you recover soon."

"Yeah, me too. When I do recover, I'd like to fly to Pondu Norax VII where we met. We can stop in and personally invite your parents to our wedding. Then we can dine at the restaurant where we met. Do you think anyone you know still works there?"

"Oh, Shane, that sounds like a good idea. My parents would love that. I haven't seen them in years. And it would be so romantic to stop in and dine where we met. I'm sure none of my friends still work there. It's been at least five years since I moved from Pondu Norax VII to Myrath. But I'd also like to stop at my old friend's house. I haven't seen

Troi in such a long time. I wonder if she'd consider being my maid of honor…or my matron of honor, if she's married now," Shanda said.

"I love you," he said as he looked up at her beautiful smile.

"Oh, Shane, I love *you.*"

The Tiffan Siram Galactic War raged across the galaxy. Space battles and turbulent worlds were numerous. It would take years to complete the war. The Third Tiffan Siram Empire fought hard, but the Thraxians and their allies knew they must win the war. For if they failed to do so, then it would be an end to their freedom. But they had a hope. They had something to fight for that was much more important than their freedom. They fought for God. They fought to recirculate the Word of God throughout the galaxy. Spreading the gospel would be a major battle in itself. Not everyone would accept it, but at least they had the chance to make that decision once again. Before the re-discovery of the Bible, they did not have that chance. Many new things would come out of this finding—many good things. What treasure could be worth more than the Will of God in a galaxy filled with sin? People would have the opportunity to accept Jesus as their Savior. After the Holy Bible was finished being distributed throughout the galaxy, more people would discover the failure of the Universal Expanse Church. It would slowly wither away like a flower in autumn.

Many AGTs pulled into the church parking lot. There was much excitement and discussion about the wedding as the people walked toward the church entrance. The large stone building was not far from the Lysith Palace. It was newly decorated with a large, empty cross to represent Christ's crucifixion and resurrection—which they were not aware of before the re-discovery of the Bible. Ushers sat the people in the sanctuary. The large room was detailed with many wedding designs. Pew bows of blue, beige, and mauve were fixed along the aisle. Shane stood at the end of the aisle. His long, brown hair stood out against the white tuxedo. A blue boutonniere was pinned to the front of his tuxedo. As he scanned the growing crowd, he became nervous. Standing beside Shane was Moro, his best man. Beside Moro stood Desinarr and Tharakon as groomsmen. On the left side of the aisle stood Troi, the maid of honor. Her long, curly, black hair trailed down her back. She wore a mauve dress with lace fringes. Next to her was

Tereen and Ameriss as bride's maids. They also wore mauve dresses. Each one of them held a small bouquet of flowers. Shane looked up at Pastor Renlin and smiled. The pastor wore a blue suit that almost matched his skin color. He stood calmly on the sanctuary platform.

The audience grew quiet as the wedding music started. The bride appeared at the entrance of the sanctuary. She wore an elaborate white gown decorated with lace. Attached to her small head-piece was a white veil. Next to the head-piece, a single red rose stood out beautifully against her blond hair. Her flowing, blond hair trailed down her back. The crown of her breasts protruded from the low-cut design. A pearl necklace was positioned about her neck. The gown's open backside was a corset-style with a series of crisscrossed laces. An array of pearls lined the back of her gown. Extending behind her was the gown's long train. In her hand, she held a bouquet of brilliant blue and mauve flowers. A hint of baby's breath was spread through the radiant flowers. Lace ribbons and pearls projected down from the bouquet. Emitting from the flowers was a sweet aroma.

Her father stood beside her. As they started down the aisle in step with the wedding music, Shanda saw Ariel sitting in the audience. She also saw some of her old friends from her home planet. She noticed some of Shane's old friends from years ago. Then Shanda saw her mother and other relatives. She tried hard to hold back her tears, but they started flowing. Ahead, she saw Shane in his white tuxedo. He looked fabulous. When she came to a stop next to Shane, her father let her arm go and sat down next to her mother. When the music ceased, Shane took Shanda's hand, and together they walked up the steps to the platform. Their wedding party followed in behind them. They looked at each other and then turned to face the pastor.

"We are gathered here today in the presence of God for the marriage of Shane Aslat and Shanda Rubine. Let us pray together.

"Dear Father in heaven, we stand before you on this beautiful day to join these two in the bonds of holy matrimony. Give them Your grace and love. Fill their union with the flowing power of the Holy Spirit. Lead them in the ways of peace, love, and righteousness. Dear God, please guide them and enrich their lives. May the vows they are about to take be kept holy and pure. May they have fruitful lives now and in the life to come. Listen to our prayer in the cherished name of Jesus Christ, who taught us the Lord's Prayer:

"Our Father who art in heaven,
Hallowed be thy name.
Thy kingdom come.
Thy will be done on earth as it is in heaven.
Give us this day our daily bread.
And forgive us our debts, as we forgive our debtors.
And lead us not into temptation, but deliver us from evil.
For thine is the kingdom, and the power, and the
glory, forever. Amen."

Pastor Renlin administered the reciting of their vows. "Shane Aslat, do you solemnly declare that you take to yourself and acknowledge as wife Shanda Rubine, here present, and do you promise that you will, with the gracious help of God, love, and maintain her, live with her in the holy bonds of marriage according to God's ordinance, and never forsake her so long as you both shall live?"

"I do," he said.

"And Shanda Rubine, do you solemnly declare that you take to yourself and acknowledge as your husband Shane Aslat, here present, and do you promise that you will, with the gracious help of God, love, honor, and obey him in all things lawful, live with him in the holy bonds of marriage according to God's ordinance, and never forsake him so long as you both shall live?"

"I do," she said.

When they were finished, Auranaxis's little son brought the rings onto the platform. They picked the rings up from the pillow and placed them on each others fingers.

"I now pronounce you, Shane and Shanda, husband and wife, in the Name of the Father and of the Son and of the Holy Spirit."

Shane and Shanda walked over to a candelabrum. They both reached for the two lit candles. After lighting the candle in the center, they blew out the ones they held and replaced them in their respective holders. They looked at the single flame. Shane lifted Shanda's veil over her head. Her beautiful eyes were traced with eyeliner. Her cheeks were blush. Shane took her in his arms and kissed her sweet lips. It was a long kiss.

APPENDICES

CHRONOLOGY OF EMPERORS AND EMPRESSES OF THE IMPERIUM AND OTHER LEADERS OF THE TIFFAN SIRAM GALAXY

First Tiffan Siram Empire
(Clans of Raatoris)

1.	Saadi Duelthine (Nesb Clan)	7109—7142	33 years
2.	Barlious Vescove (Nesb Clan)	7142—7169	27 years
3.	Lee Manic (Amonis Clan)	7169—7187	18 years
4.	Pherin Omnell (Rhen Clan)	7187—7192	5 years
5.	Torell Sinthis (Amonis Clan)	7192—7214	22 years
6.	Ellis Shirenaught (Thesila Clan)	7214—7246	32 years
7.	Nerell Cowenth (Nesb Clan)	7246—7291	45 years
	Interregnum	7291—7361	70 years

House of Althore

8.	Alexander I	7361—7386	25 years
9.	Vincent I	7386—7403	17 years
10.	Thomas	7403—7409	6 years
11.	Abott	7409—7412	3 years
12.	Alexander II	7412—7422	10 years
13.	Ivan	7422—7424	2 years
14.	Boris	7424—7430	6 years
15.	Lisgher	7430—7435	5 years
16.	Vincent II	7435—7438	3 years
17.	Vincent III	7438—7448	10 years

House of Usell

18.	Stephen	7448—7464	16 years
19.	Dekull	7464—7498	34 years
20.	Muisquire	7498—7514	16 years
21.	Erla	7514—7524	10 years
22.	Usio'lei	7524—7551	27 years
23.	Taunera	7551—7564	13 years
24.	Flangel	7564—7570	6 years
25.	Anyx	7570—7585	15 years
26.	Ebart	7585—7596	11 years

Vanest Dynasty

27.	Shellis	7596—7613	17 years
28.	Amandan	7613—7633	20 years
29.	Aaron	7633—7654	21 years
30.	Shandis	7654—7676	22 years
31.	Garnith	7676—7699	23 years
32.	Arriel	7699—7724	25 years
33.	Troi	7724—7752	28 years
34.	Racio	7752—7784	32 years
35.	Robinell	7784—7800	16 years
36.	April	7800—7820	20 years
37.	Berkalin	7820—7834	14 years

House of El-Ryoth

38.	Geos	7834—7839	5 years
39.	Pharness	7839—7842	3 years

First Republic
(Presidents)

40.	James Ooit	7842—7847	5 years
41.	Sinarr Aas'ott	7847—7852	5 years
42.	Sampson Marne	7852—7857	5 years
43.	Morris Tuvell	7857—7862	5 years
44.	Thomas Ducord	7862—7867	5 years

45.	Stephen Not'reen	7867—7872	5 years
46.	Fascinell Obit	7872—7877	5 years
47.	Alexander Sardik	7877—7882	5 years
48.	Niishah Vioneel	7882—7887	5 years
49.	Olen Radell	7887—7892	5 years
	Interregnum	7892—7920	28 years

First Tiffan Siram Empire (Restored)
Age of the Tyrants
House of Axe

50.	Quarrel	7920—7970	50 years
51.	Duelous	7970—8000	30 years
52.	Zorvhel	8000—8024	24 years
53.	Boris	8024—8061	37 years
54.	Celltii	8061—8101	40 years
55.	Wideve	8101—8124	23 years
56.	Blackie	8124—8142	18 years
57.	Tyranis	8142—8170	28 years
58.	Abagott	8170—8200	30 years
59.	Garth	8200—8241	41 years
60.	Torell I	8241—8249	8 years
61.	Torell II	8249—8269	20 years
62.	Torell III	8269—8284	15 years
63.	Torell IV	8284—8286	2 years
64.	Ameed II	8286—8322	36 years
65.	Torell V	8322—8347	25 years
66.	Ingster	8347—8365	18 years
67.	Abridith I	8365—8382	17 years
68.	Anexious I	8382—8439	57 years
69.	Anexious II	8439—8502	63 years
70.	Abridith II	8502—8549	47 years
71.	Reignaught	8549—8604	55 years
72.	Priscilla	8604—8610	6 years

Second Republic
(Presidents)

73.	Priscilla Axe	8610—8615	5 years
74.	Victor Hanon	8615—8620	5 years
75.	Amon Nez-Onnis	8620—8625	5 years

First Tiffan Siram Empire (Restored)
House of Morr

76.	Arris	8625—8657	32 years
77.	Narell	8657—8672	15 years
78.	On'terris	8672—8702	30 years
79.	Sandithist	8702—8727	25 years
80.	Juliser II	8727—8756	29 years
81.	Rogen	8756—8769	13 years
82.	Bashsiahn	8769—8781	12 years
83.	Trevor	8781—8833	52 years
84.	Alpiira	8833—8880	47 years
85.	Lighren	8880—8898	18 years
86.	Adexin I	8898—8913	15 years
87.	Q'eenell III	8913—8930	17 years
88.	Adexin II	8930—8940	10 years
89.	Simonson	8940—8952	12 years
90.	Adexin III	8952—8968	16 years
91.	Onantious IV	8968—8989	21 years
92.	Adexin IV	8989—9000	11 years
93.	Onantious V	9000—9009	9 years
94.	Onantious VI	9009—9012	3 years
95.	Adexin V	9012—9019	7 years
96.	Willentis	9019—9029	10 years
97.	Onantious VIII	9029—9037	8 years
98.	Onantious IX	9037—9067	30 years
99.	Frevinson	9067—9079	12 years
100.	Onantious X	9079—9136	57 years
101.	Allious	9136—9206	70 years

The Regency

| 102. | Alexander Tupell | 9206—9218 | 12 years |
| 103. | Trevor Noothis | 9218—9225 | 7 years |

Acern Dynasty

104.	Edron	9225—9252	27 years
105.	Morton	9252—9284	32 years
106.	Celin	9284—9305	21 years
107.	Bechra	9305	2 months

House of Oldmill

108.	Murry	9305—9347	42 years
109.	Anon	9347—9382	35 years
110.	Sheth	9382—9409	27 years
111.	Tross	9409—9460	51 years
112.	Lisa	9460—9494	34 years
113.	Farris IV	9494—9508	14 years
114.	Mokurk	9508—9540	32 years
115.	Jen	9540—9567	27 years
116.	Daniel	9567—9607	40 years
117.	Aaron I	9607—9660	53 years
118.	Elington	9660—9661	1 year
119.	Aaron II	9661—9673	12 years
120.	Victoria	9673—9705	32 years
121.	Janis	9705—9722	17 years
122.	Destiny	9722—9779	57 years
123.	Arrnith	9779—9803	24 years

Era of the Wise
House of Pearl

124.	Wenell	9803—9829	26 years
125.	Mike	9829—9841	12 years
126.	Alex	9841—9854	13 years
127.	Isperr	9854—9869	15 years
128.	Trina	9869—9889	20 years

129.	Angel	9889—9911	22 years
130.	James	9911—9924	13 years
131.	Rixell	9924—9942	18 years
132.	Ben	9942—9982	40 years
133.	Harris	9982—9998	16 years

House of Ali-Sheth

134.	Thomas	9998—10000	2 years
135.	Adrian	10000—10003	3 years

Restoration of House of Pearl

136.	Levi	10003—10018	15 years
137.	Max	10018—10055	37 years
138.	Tori	10055—10063	8 years

House of Phillips

139.	Duke	10063—10097	34 years
140.	Jaremm	10097—10124	27 years

House of Gibson

141.	Rabecca	10124—10149	25 years
142.	Dion	10149—10196	47 years
143.	Elonis	10196—10203	7 years
144.	Tibettis	10203—10242	39 years
145.	Asanthria	10242—10254	12 years
146.	Yem-El	10254—10273	19 years

Third Republic
(Presidents)

147.	George Rell	10273—10278	5 years
148.	Amoss Naught	10278—10283	5 years
149.	Chester Royatt	10283—10288	5 years
150.	Earl Simon	10288—10293	5 years

First Tiffan Siram Empire (Restored)
House of Stone

151.	Ebon I	10293—10309	16 years
152.	Ebon II	10309—10316	7 years
153.	Asher	10316—10318	2 years

Cove Dynasty

154.	Berella	10318—10321	3 years
155.	Hermis	10321	1 week
156.	Foxter	10321	2 days

House of Quest

157.	Unis	10321	2 months
158.	Adorr II	10321	3 hours

Fourth Republic
(Presidents)

159.	Emitt Fer'nell	10321—10326	5 years
160.	Perry Sage	10326—10331	5 years

First Tiffan Siram Empire (Restored)
House of Raspbarr

161.	Luke I	10331—10343	12 years
162.	Charles	10343—10366	23 years
163.	Hanorr	10366—10391	25 years
164.	Lex	10391—10408	17 years
165.	Ibingwell	10408—10411	3 years
166.	Meso'neal	10411—10421	10 years
167.	Wesachia	10421—10422	1 year
168.	Luke IV	10422—10424	2 years
169.	Solomon I	10424—10442	18 years
170.	Solomon II	10442—10458	16 years
171.	Eric IX	10458—10473	15 years
172.	Luke VII	10473—10477	4 years

173.	Troy XVIII	10477—10489	12 years
174.	Solomon V	10489—10512	23 years
175.	Troy XIX	10512—10519	7 years
176.	Richard VIII	10519—10529	10 years
177.	Troy XX	10529—10537	8 years
178.	Roger VI	10537—10543	6 years
179.	Roger VII	10543—10555	12 years
180.	Thessor I	10555—10585	30 years
181.	Zonorr	10585—10590	5 years
182.	Solomon IX	10590—10598	8 years
183.	Thessor IV	10598—10640	42 years
184.	Xarrin'is	10640—10689	49 years
185.	Newton II	10689—10749	60 years
186.	Tawn	10749—10761	12 years
187.	Faradd	10761—10830	69 years
188.	Taar VI	10830—10847	17 years
189.	Transurr	10847—10850	3 years
190.	Elama	10850—10862	12 years

Fifth Republic
(Presidents)

191.	Edward Stevenson	10862—10864	2 years
192.	Aman Evens	10864—10869	5 years
193.	Richard Horton	10869—10874	5 years
194.	Pierre Au'max	10874—10879	5 years
195.	Vincent Poridine	10879—10884	5 years
196.	Albert Webb	10884—10889	5 years
197.	Nancy Bright	10889—10894	5 years
198.	Norman Shores	10894—10899	5 years
199.	Aam Rellis	10899—10904	5 years
200.	Mike Harbor	10904—10909	5 years

First Tiffan Siram Empire (Restored)
House of Mayport

201.	Markous	10909—10912	3 years
202.	Micheal	10912—10915	3 years
203.	Robert	10915—10918	3 years

204.	Douglas	10918—10930	12 years
205.	Daryl	10930	5 minutes
206.	Marcia	10930—10933	3 years
207.	Joseph	10933—10944	11 years

The Regency

208.	Sirshell Alps	10944—10978	34 years
209.	Zach Mellington	10978—11005	27 years

Era of the Thraxians
House of Teserane

210.	Athix'bothan	11005—11209	204 years
211.	Sterlinanian	11209—11341	132 years
212.	Roothis'alb	11341—11641	300 years
213.	Xexineoul	11641—11908	267 years
214.	Technestex	11908—12097	189 years
215.	Biisell-Taunbotsh	12097—12409	312 years
216.	Foosloopchicio	12409—12678	269 years
217.	Onnadoristonson	12678—12894	216 years
218.	Thurmyvezzabeoch	12894—13208	314 years
	Interregnum	13208—13209	1 year

First Tiffan Siram Empire (Restored)
House of Bayset

219.	Ellis	13209	3 months
	Galactic Revolution	13209—13756	547 years

Sixth Republic
(Presidents)

220.	Andrew Tama	13756—13761	5 years
221.	Raven Bluemass	13761—13766	5 years
222.	Lech Rowen	13766—13771	5 years

Seventh Republic
(Presidents)

223.	William Abs	13771—13775	4 years
224.	Ais Mott	13775—13779	4 years
225.	Leon Chilian	13779—13783	4 years
226.	Rex Adams	13783—13787	4 years
227.	Stuart Kaubyrr	13787—13791	4 years
228.	Kelly Greenfields	13791—13795	4 years
229.	Alexander Sights	13795—13799	4 years
230.	Winston Sands	13799—13803	4 years
231.	Anthony Foxflight	13803—13807	4 years
232.	Tina Meadows	13807—13811	4 years
233.	Thomas Allen	13811—13815	4 years
234.	Oloss Cantell	13815—13819	4 years
235.	Kenneth Nott	13819—13823	4 years
	Interregnum	13823—13926	103 years

Second Tiffan Siram Empire
House of Northtower

236.	Adarr	13926—13951	25 years
237.	Malice	13951—13983	32 years
238.	Dude	13983—14001	18 years
239.	Cydan	14001—14048	47 years
240.	Tyran	14048—14064	16 years
241.	Clyde	14064—14089	25 years
242.	Thorr	14089—14115	26 years
243.	Cyshon	14115—14138	23 years
244.	Notorr	14138—14172	34 years
245.	Faction	14172—14213	41 years
246.	Toothan	14213—14242	29 years
247.	Aaron	14242—14275	33 years

House of Cladstone

248.	Alinyf	14275—14291	16 years
249.	Noriss	14291—14316	25 years

250.	Richard	14316—14333	17 years
251.	Darsen	14333—14354	21 years
252.	Glenison	14354—14386	32 years
253.	Michler	14386—14414	28 years
254.	Torastra	14414—14428	14 years
255.	Newtjama	14428—14447	19 years
256.	Serinis	14447—14477	30 years
257.	Pownrell	14477—14493	16 years

House of Arc

258.	Loosern	14493—14535	42 years
259.	Michen	14535—14547	12 years
260.	Gabellis	14547—14559	12 years
261.	Trudon	14559—14567	8 years
262.	Apriss	14567—14596	29 years
263.	Sepheenis	14596—14623	27 years
264.	Wendalynn	14623—14657	34 years
265.	Bradamorr	14657—14711	54 years

House of Tymor

266.	Alice	14711—14726	15 years
267.	Chriss	14726—14739	13 years
268.	Venis	14739—14749	10 years
269.	Ytersill	14749—14760	11 years
270.	Narlen	14760—14783	23 years
271.	Laa'dem	14783—14825	42 years
272.	Semadian	14825—14843	18 years
273.	Wesley	14843—14870	27 years
274.	Stronis	14870—14906	36 years
275.	Lebrian	14906—14958	52 years
276.	Wyotiff	14958—14995	37 years
	Interregnum	14995—15000	5 years

New Galactic Order
Galactic Government
(Leaders)

277.	Arrionis Forsyth I	15000—15034	34 years
278.	Arrionis Forsyth II	15034—15056	22 years
279.	Alex Rytecoff	15056—15077	21 years
280.	Straton Arnious	15077—15088	11 years

Third Tiffan Siram Empire (Name Restored)

281.	Boris Anathor	15088—

Terminology Glossary

Chapter references are where the term first appears in the novel.
(Some terms may contain slight spoilers.)

A

Aarian - (Chapter 4) He was the freelance captain of a space freighter ship named *Aarian's Freighter.* Aarian had gray hair.

Aarian's Freighter - (Chapter 4) A space freighter ship owned by a freelance captain named Aarian.

Abbitarr - (Chapter 10) A Third Tiffan Siram Empire battleship under the leadership of Captain Ertlees. The *Abbitarr* was destroyed when the captain attacked a gas mining asteroid in the Ythorn Asteroid Mass, which caused an extremely large explosion.

Adarr - (Chapter 6) He was the business partner of Aarian on *Aarian's Freighter* until his death.

Age of the Masses - (Chapter 2) It was a reference to a time when all the clans on the planet Raatoris had many disputes.

Age of the Tyrants - (Chapter 3) It was a time during the First Tiffan Siram Empire when the House of Axe was in power. They were tyrants to the citizens of the galaxy for approximately 690 years, from the year 7920 to the year 8610. Their reign ended when the last ruler, Empress Priscilla Axe transitioned the governance to the Second Republic. She was the first president of the Second Republic.

Almonis Tarque - (Chapter 8) A planet that was the seat of the Thraxian Government.

Almoss - (Chapter 3) An old-fashioned town on the planet Myrath.

Alnor - (Chapter 1) A planet located in the Telneth Star System. Alnor was destroyed during the Telfire Wars. It was located within the Galactic Government / Tiffan Siram Empire's jurisdiction.

Ameriss - (Chapter 10) She was a Thraxian who lived in the city of Shenix Falls on the planet Almonis Tarque. Ameriss had white hair. She was good friends with Shanda Rubine.

Amminar - (Chapter 5) He was a Galactic Government official who betrayed the leader, Straton Arnious and his other dignitaries and advisors. Amminar poisoned them to help Boris Anathor become emperor and restore the government name as the Third Tiffan Siram Empire.

Amonis Clan - (Chapter 2) One of the Notable Clans on the planet Raatoris.

Amonith - (Chapter 7) He was a shuttle pilot who lived on the planet Obrah.

Amveries - (Chapter 10) A planet that was greatly affected by the Tiffan Siram Galactic War. Amveries was located within the Galactic Government / Tiffan Siram Empire's jurisdiction.

Anathor, Emperor Boris - (Chapter 5) He was the emperor of the Third Tiffan Siram Empire after a hostile takeover of the Galactic Government and its leader, Straton Arnious.

Ancient Prophets - (Chapter 8) A poem by Remyw Yort.

Ancient Raatoris - (Chapter 2) A period of time on the planet Raatoris when it was controlled by the Scyllian Clan.

Anti-gravitational Transport (AGT) - (Chapter 4) An anti-gravitational land craft.

Archineel - (Chapter 2) It was the official language of the First Tiffan Siram Empire, after it had been changed from Nesbeoch. Archineel was used in communications between most of the planets of the galaxy. The origin of Archineel was from the old, destroyed planet Seelious, which was destroyed when a drifting satellite collided into it.

Arnious, Straton - (Chapter 2) He lived on the planet Ishtorb. Straton was the fourth leader of the Galactic Government after the implementation of the New Galactic Order. He had black and gray hair.

Aslat, Shane - (Chapter 1) He was from the planet Elbi, which was destroyed during the Telfire Wars. Shane's parents were killed there. During the evacuation, he was separated from his brother. Shane was one point eight meters tall. He had green eyes and long, brown hair. Shane's left ear was pierced. His girlfriend was Shanda Rubine. Shane acquired a spaceship named *Star Crystal.*

Auranaxis - (Chapter 8) He was a Thraxian who lived on the planet Almonis Tarque. Auranaxis was an officer in the Thraxian military during the Tiffan Siram Galactic War. He was bald on top of his head and had long, white hair in the back. Auranaxis was the father of a young Thraxian boy. He also had a dog named Teraster. Auranaxis befriended Shane Aslat and Shanda Rubine while searching for the treasure.

Axithorp - (Chapter 7) Large, green creatures with sharp teeth that looked more fierce than they actually were.

B

Bartu - (Chapter 1) A planet located in the Telneth Star System. Bartu was destroyed during the Telfire Wars. It was located within the Galactic Government / Tiffan Siram Empire's jurisdiction.

Bassin, Moro - (Chapter 7) He was a star crystal miner and later an inventory control specialist. Moro had gray hair. He owned a spaceship named *Star Crystal*.

Bathannia's World - (Chapter 1) A remote planet known for its intoxication joints and gambling facilities. Bathannia's World was located within the Galactic Government / Tiffan Siram Empire's jurisdiction.

Both - (Chapter 10) He was an officer in the Third Tiffan Siram Empire military. Both was the lead officer of the *Abbitarr*.

C

Calazen - (Chapter 10) He was a Devrakian representative to the Thraxian Government.

D

Delbis Salias - (Chapter 10) A planet that was located outside of the Galactic Government / Tiffan Siram Empire's jurisdiction.

Desinarr - (Chapter 10) He was a Thraxian who lived on the planet Almonis Tarque. Desinarr was the Thraxian Government administrator. He had white hair.

Devrakian - (Chapter 10) A short species with gray skin and large red eyes. A series of small ripples covered their bald heads. Devrakians spoke with reverberating tones.

Duelthine, Saadi - (Chapter 2) He was from the Nesb Clan on the planet Raatoris. Saadi became the first emperor of the First Tiffan Siram Empire. He was responsible for seating the imperial throne on the planet Sulluth.

E

Early First Tiffan Siram Empire - (Chapter 2) The time period when the First Tiffan Siram Empire was occupied by the Notable Clans, from the year 7109 to the year 7291.

Elbi - (Chapter 1) A planet located in the Telneth Star System. Elbi was destroyed during the Telfire Wars. It was located within the Galactic Government / Tiffan Siram Empire's jurisdiction.

Emperor Boris Anathor - (*See* Anathor, Emperor Boris)

Emperor Semadian Tymor - (*See* Tymor, Emperor Semadian)

Emperor Tulli - (Chapter 3) He was the emperor of the Tulli Realm with territory around the town of Almoss on the planet Myrath. Emperor Tulli was a warrior who conquered the small village during the early colonization of Myrath. He resided in the Tulli Castle on Mount Amor, which overlooked the town of Almoss. Emperor Tulli had gray hair. He kept a harem of women in the Tulli Castle for his pleasure.

Era of the Thraxians - (Chapter 8) It was a time during the First Tiffan Siram Empire when the House of Teserane was in power. Era of the Thraxians was the first and only time a non-human race was in power in the imperium. The Thraxians ruled for approximately 2203 years, from the year 11005 to the year 13208. Eventually, the humans forced the Thraxians to step down and a period of interregnum followed.

Ertlees, Captain - (Chapter 10) He was an officer in the Third Tiffan Siram Empire military. Ertlees was the captain of the *Abbitarr*.

Expeditionary Journals - (Chapter 8) A series of journals from a well known galactic traveler named Vincent Ryineos.

F

Feenith - (Chapter 1) An old city on the planet Selnaan.

First Tiffan Siram Empire - (Chapter 1) A galactic empire that was founded in the year 7109 by the Notable Clans of Raatoris. The duration of First Tiffan Siram Empire was approximately 6100 years; however, there were interruptions many times with interregnums and multiple republics. It ended with the Galactic Revolution. The seat of the First Tiffan Siram Empire was originally on the planet Raatoris, but later moved to the planet Sulluth.

Futuristic Dreams - (Chapter 8) A poem by the legendary poet Remyw Yort.

G

Galactic Economics Exchange Council (GEEC) - (Chapter 5) An organization established in the year 14831 by Emperor Semadian Tymor during the Second Tiffan Siram Empire. The Galactic Economics Exchange Council was founded to help the galactic economy, but many years later, under the New Galactic Order, the system was filled with corruption and a tool for control through digital currency.

Galactic Government - (Chapter 1) A government formed in the year 15000 by a group of people from the New Galactic Order. The Galactic Government was a controversial government with much overreach and a tyrannical, dystopian control. Its jurisdiction was a vast portion of the Tiffan Siram Galaxy, but not the entire galaxy. The seat of the Galactic Government was on the planet Ishtorb.

Galactic Government Troops - (Chapter 1) Galactic Government military officers.

Galaxy's High Degree of Wanted Criminals - (Chapter 7) A television program that featured the galaxy's supposed high degree of wanted criminals in the hopes that the citizens of the galaxy watching the program would help in their capture. Unfortunately, the dystopian government included non-criminals who dissented from the government's political views.

H

House of Teserane - (Chapter 8) A family of Thraxians who ruled during the First Tiffan Siram Empire. It was known as the Era of the Thraxians with nine different emperors over 2203 years.

House of Tymor - (Chapter 5) A family who ruled during the Second

Tiffan Siram Empire with eleven different emperors over 284 years.

I

Imperial Throne - (Chapter 2) A reference to the seat of government in any of the Tiffan Siram Empires.

Ineffective Life - (Chapter 8) A poem by Remyw Yort.

intoxication joint - (Chapter 1) A drinking establishment.

Ironclad - (Chapter 8) He was the captain of the sail ship *Maritime Maiden.*

Ishtorb - (Chapter 2) A planet that was the seat of the Galactic Government and the Third Tiffan Siram Empire.

K

Kelv Wesnith Synod - (Chapter 3) A synod that came to exist in the year 8217, during the Age of the Tyrants. The Kelv Wesnith Synod assembled together on the planet Troth to draft and create an acknowledgment of faith in the one true religion.

Kelv Wesnith Synod Acknowledgment of Faith - (Chapter 3) An acknowledgment of faith drafted by the Kelv Wesnith Synod in the year 8217.

L

Leenith - (Chapter 6) He was the assistant minister for the main Universal Expanse Church on the planet Troth.

Life's Sorrow - (Chapter 8) A poem by Remyw Yort.

lightspeed-plus - (Chapter 1) A general term used to reference spaceship speeds beyond that of light.

Lost Scroll, The - (Chapter 1) It was a reference to The Stolen Scroll that had been passed down through the generations of the Naith family and had became lost. The search for The Lost Scroll was minimal.

Lysith Palace - (Chapter 10) A tall building in the great city of Shenix Falls on the planet Almonis Tarque that was the seat of the Thraxian Government. The Lysith Palace was an enormous structure with many towers and spires extending into the sky, including landing platforms extending out from the towers.

M

Maritime Maiden - (Chapter 8) An old sail ship owned by a captain named Ironclad. *Maritime Maiden's* homeport was the town of Thisilia on the Slave Sea of the planet Myrath.

Metrocity - (Chapter 1) A city on the planet Yaraden.

Misquee Shores - (Chapter 7) A city on the planet Obrah.

Mount Amor - (Chapter 3) A mountain near the town of Almoss on the planet Myrath.

Morrison - (Chapter 8) He lived in the port town of Thisilia on the planet Myrath. Morrison had gray hair. He ran a horse stable business in Thisilia.

Myrath - (Chapter 3) An antiquated planet located outside of the Galactic Government's jurisdiction.

N

Naith, Allio - (Chapter 2) He was an engineer on the planet Onorra. Allio was known for finding the Stolen Scroll.

Namaas Forest - (Chapter 1) A vast forest that covered one third of the planet Raatoris.

Nesb Clan - (Chapter 2) One of the Notable Clans on the planet Raatoris.

Nesbeoch - (Chapter 2) The language of the Nesb Clan. Nesbeoch became the official language of the planet Raatoris.

New Galactic Order - (Chapter 2) A federation of planets controlled by the Galactic Government with its authoritarian power and control.

Norba - (Chapter 3) He was an aide for Emperor Tulli.

Notable Clans - (Chapter 2) A group of clans from the planet Raatoris that came together and founded the First Tiffan Siram Empire, which put an end to the Age of the Masses. The Notable Clans included the Nesb Clan, the Amonis Clan, the Rhen Clan, and the Thesila Clan.

Nottoran, Commander - (Chapter 10) He was a Thraxian commander in the Thraxian military. Nottoran's regiment fought on the planet Amveries during the Tiffan Siram Galactic War. He had white hair.

O

Obrah - (Chapter 4) A planet located on the border and within the Galactic Government's jurisdiction.

Ojenis Temples - (Chapter 1) They were temples located in the Namaas Forest on the planet Raatoris. The Ojenis Temples were built by the Scyllian Clan to preserve a majestic treasure they had discovered in the Namaas Forest.

Onorra - (Chapter 2) A planet where Allio Naith worked as an engineer. Onorra was located within the Galactic Government / Tiffan Siram Empire's jurisdiction.

P

Piross - (Chapter 2) He was an undercover agent for the Galactic Government. Piross was bald.

Pondu Norax VII - (Chapter 3) A planet located outside of the Galactic Government / Tiffan Siram Empire's jurisdiction.

Port Fae - (Chapter 8) A port town on the Slave Sea on the planet Myrath.

R

Raatoris - (Chapter 1) A planet that had approximately one third of its surface covered by the Namaas Forest. The First Tiffan Siram Empire was founded on Raatoris and was the original seat of the empire. The Imperial Throne was later moved to the planet Sulluth by the first emperor. Toward the end of the First Tiffan Siram Empire, before the Galactic Revolution, Raatoris was set aside as a memorial planet and abandoned. Although Raatoris was within the Galactic Government / Tiffan Siram Empire's jurisdiction, the planet eventually had been forgotten.

Raatoris Conference - (Chapter 2) A conference that was held in the year 7108 on the planet Raatoris by a group of noble people from each of the clans on that planet. The group, known as the Notable Clans, made many important decisions during the conference, including making their official language Nesbeoch and to form the First Tiffan Siram Empire.

***Reigning On You (Return of* Thee)** - (Chapter 8) A poem by Remyw Yort.

Renlin, Pastor - (Chapter 10) He was a Thraxian pastor who lived on the planet Almonis Tarque. Pastor Renlin had white hair.

Resofain Clan - (Chapter 2) A clan on the planet Raatoris. The Resofain Clan existed after the Scyllian Clan and before the Notable Clans. They were known for their discovery of a scroll left behind by the Scyllian Clan. The Resofain Clan put the scroll into a Resofain museum.

Rhen Clan - (Chapter 2) One of the Notable Clans on the planet Raatoris.

Romison, Harris - (Chapter 8) He was a famous wise man. Harris wrote the *Wisdom Chronicles.*

Rubine, Shanda - (Chapter 1) She was originally from the planet Pondu Norax VII. Shanda lived in the town of Almoss on the planet Myrath. She had long, blond hair. Shanda's boyfriend was Shane Aslat. She was best friends with Troi.

Ryineos, Vincent - (Chapter 8) He was a galactic traveler known for his *Expeditionary Journals.*

Rytoorian Asteroid Mass - (Chapter 7) A group of asteroids where a star crystal mining operation was located.

S

Sands of Time, The - (Chapter 8) A poem by Remyw Yort.

Scyllian Clan - (Chapter 1) One of the first known clans on Ancient Raatoris in the year 4863. The Scyllian Clan had discovered a majestic treasure in the Namaas Forest in the year 5181 and build the Ojenis Temples in the forest to preserve it in. The clan mysteriously disappeared from the planet in the year 5612, but left behind evidence of the treasure and the Ojenis Temples, including a scroll. After their disappearance, there were still people on Raatoris, however, none of them were yet organized into other clans yet.

Second Tiffan Siram Empire - (Chapter 2) A galactic empire that was founded in the year 13926 by the House of Northtower. The duration of Second Tiffan Siram Empire was approximately 1069 years. It ended with an interregnum just before the New Galactic Order and the formation of the Galactic Government. The seat of the Second Tiffan Siram Empire was on the planet Sulluth.

Seelious - (Chapter 2) A planet that was destroyed when a drifting satellite collided into it. Seelious was the origin of the main language in the Tiffan Siram Galaxy.

Selnaan - (Chapter 1) A planet where an annual historic art festival was held. Selnaan was located within the Galactic Government / Tiffan Siram Empire's jurisdiction.

Shallum Ibner - (Chapter 1) A planet located in the Telneth Star System. Shallum Ibner was destroyed during the Telfire Wars. It was located within the Galactic Government / Tiffan Siram Empire's jurisdiction.

Shenix Falls - (Chapter 10) A city on the planet Almonis Tarque where the seat of the Thraxian Government was located.

Shenix Falls Medical Facility - (Chapter 10) A hospital in the city of Shenix Falls on the planet Almonis Tarque.

Sheth - (Chapter 1) Many orphans were relocated to Sheth during the Telfire Wars. Sheth was located within the Galactic Government / Tiffan Siram Empire's jurisdiction.

Slave Sea - (Chapter 3) A large sea on the planet Myrath.

SR Series Robot - (Chapter 4) Robots that had been manufactured on the planet Yaraden.

star crystal (mineral) - (Chapter 7) A valuable mineral that was mined in certain asteroids.

***Star Crystal* (spaceship)** - (Chapter 7) A spaceship initially owned by Moro Bassin. Moro gave the *Star Crystal* to Shane Aslat.

Stolen Scroll, The - (Chapter 2) It was a reference to the scroll that had been stolen from a Resofain museum. The Stolen Scroll was found on another planet in the year 6946 by Allio Naith. The scroll itself told the story of a majestic treasure discovered by the Scyllian Clan of Raatoris and the Ojenis Temples they had built to preserve the treasure in.

Stoughe, Adrex - (Chapter 3) He was a Universal Expansionist. In 8360, Adrex Stoughe composed the *Stoughe Creed.* He died a martyr.

Stoughe Creed - (Chapter 3) It was composed by Adrex Stoughe in the year 8360. The *Stoughe Creed* was a summary of the *Kelv Wesnith Synod Acknowledgment of Faith.* The creed consisted of five elements of canon law: the Creator made everything, the Creator has the power to perform anything that He wishes, He is in control of everything at all times, He is the All-seeing Eye, and His spiritual creatures should love Him and each other and be wise unto death.

Sulluth - (Chapter 2) A planet that became the seat of the First and Second Tiffan Siram Empires. The first emperor of the imperium, Saadi Duelthine, was responsible for moving the Imperial Throne from Raatoris to Sulluth. However, the seat of the Third Tiffan Siram Empire was located on the planet Ishtorb.

Sypron Swamp - (Chapter 9) A swamp on the planet Toris, formerly named Raatoris.

T

Tarofain - (Chapter 6) A species known for their extreme height of approximately three meters tall.

Telfire Wars - (Chapter 1) A series of wars that erupted in the Telneth Star System in the year 15073 when the people demanded that the system's space freight monopoly be broken up. The conflict was originally between the original freight company and new freight companies that had formed. Eventually, the conflict shifted to the freight companies against people hauling their own freight. With the companies firing weapons at the civilians and rampant revenge, the wars soon escalated out of control. Freight insurance rose drastically and the Galactic Government chose not to be involved in the dispute. One of the larger space freight companies mysteriously came across several massive nuclear weapons. Shortly after the children were evacuated, the four planets in the system, Alnor, Elbi, Bartu, and Shallum Ibner were destroyed.

Telneth Star System - (Chapter 1) A star system in the Tiffan Siram Galaxy, within the Galactic Government / Tiffan Siram Empire's jurisdiction.

Teraster - (Chapter 9) He was a dog owned by Auranaxis.

Tereen - (Chapter 10) She was a Thraxian who lived in the city of

Shenix Falls on the planet Almonis Tarque. Tereen had white hair. She was good friends with Shanda Rubine.

Terrsil - (Chapter 6) He was a shuttle pilot who worked at the Yaraden spaceport.

Tharakon - (Chapter 10) He was a dignitary for the Thraxian Government. Tharakon had white hair.

Thesila Clan - (Chapter 2) One of the Notable Clans on the planet Raatoris.

Third Tiffan Siram Empire - (Chapter 2) Another name for the Galactic Government, but wasn't officially used until Boris Anathor overthrew Straton Arnious in the year 15088. The seat of the Third Tiffan Siram Empire was on the planet Ishtorb.

Third Tiffan Siram Empire Troops - (Chapter 8) Third Tiffan Siram military officers.

Thisilia - (Chapter 3) A port town on the Slave Sea on the planet Myrath.

Thorton - (Chapter 6) He was the minister of the main Universal Expanse Church on the planet Troth.

Thraxian - (Chapter 7) A species with neon blue skin that had a whitish tone. Thraxians had white hair. They had long, course organs in the back of their heads that enabled them to expand their awareness of other beings around them. The average life span of a Thraxian was four hundred years. Most of them lived on the planet Almonis Tarque.

Thraxian Government - (Chapter 9) A government ruled by the Thraxians. The seat of the Thraxian Government was on the planet Almonis Tarque. The government headquarters were in the Lysith Palace in the great city of Shenix Falls.

Tiffan Siram Empire - (Chapter 2) A reference to any of the First, Second, or Third Tiffan Siram Empires.

Tiffan Siram Galactic War - (Chapter 9) A war between the Thraxian Government, along with their Devrakian allies, and the Third Tiffan Siram Empire and Universal Expanse Church.

Tiffan Siram Galaxy - (Chapter 2) Throughout history, much of it was controlled by the Tiffan Siram Empire and Galactic Government as well as other governments, including the Thraxian Government.

Tion, Ariel - (Chapter 1) She lived in Metrocity on the planet Yaraden. Ariel lived outside of the Galactic Government's monetary system and became a harlot to survive. Later, she was able to move outside of their jurisdiction and found a clerical job in the city of Wintress on the planet Zenbat Oddnu IV. Ariel had long, dark brown hair and blue eyes.

Toris - (Chapter 8) An abandoned and forgotten planet. Approximately one third of its surface was covered by the Namaas Forest. It was formerly known as Raatoris. Toris was located within the Galactic Government / Tiffan Siram Empire's jurisdiction.

Torra - (Chapter 1) He lived on the planet Bathannia's World. Torra was a bald warrior. He lost a very fast fighter ship to Shane Aslat in a card game.

Troi - (Chapter 3) She lived on the planet Pondu Norax VII. Troi had long, curly, black hair. She was best friends with Shanda Rubine.

Tross - (Chapter 4) He was a business partner to Aarian on *Aarian' Freighter*. Tross was an old friend with Shane Aslat from when they both lived on the planet Bathannia's World. Shane Aslat saved Tross's life once by talking a Tarofain out of killing him.

Troth - (Chapter 3) A planet where the main Universal Expanse Church was located. Troth was home to the archives that preserved ecumenical creeds, liturgical forms, and many other religious documents. It was located outside of the Galactic Government / Tiffan Siram Empire's jurisdiction.

Tulli Castle - (Chapter 3) It was a structure built on Mount Amor near the old-fashioned town of Almoss on the planet Myrath. The Tulli Castle was the seat of the Tulli Empire.

Tulli Empire - (Chapter 8) It was a local empire on the planet Myrath controlled by Emperor Tulli.

Tulli Realm - (Chapter 3) It was a reference to the Tulli Empire. The Tulli Realm was formed early in the colonization of Myrath. Its history began when the fierce warrior Tulli conquered the small village of Almoss.

Tymor, Emperor Semadian - (Chapter 5) He was an emperor of the Second Tiffan Siram Empire from the year 14825 to the year 14843. Emperor Semadian was responsible for establishing the Galactic Economics Exchange Council (GEEC) in the year 14831.

Tyrris Militia - (Chapter 1) A space gang that was known for its renegade pirates attacks on unarmed spaceships. The Tyrris Militia raided, assaulted, and stole riches from the innocent passengers. At one point, Shane Aslat belonged to the space gang.

U

Universal Expanse Church (UEC) - (Chapter 3) It was the primary religious organization in the Tiffan Siram Galaxy. The Universal Expanse Church was formed in the year 8217 when the Kelv Wesnith Synod assembled together on the planet Troth.

Universal Expansionist - (Chapter 2) A member of the Universal Expanse Church.

W

Wintress - (Chapter 7) One of the major cities on the planet Zenbat Oddnu IV.

Wisdom Chronicles - (Chapter 8) A series of published words of wisdom by Harris Romison, one of the wisest men in history.

Y

Yaraden - (Chapter 1) An industrial planet located within the Galactic Government / Tiffan Siram Empire's jurisdiction.

Yort, Remyw - (Chapter 8) He was a legendary poet. Remyw was known for poetry that moved people.

Ythorn Asteroid Mass - (Chapter 10) A group of asteroids where a gas mining operation was located. The mining operation was destroyed during the Tiffan Siram Galactic War when the Third Tiffan Siram Empire battleship *Abbitarr* fired on the mine, causing a massive explosion that also destroyed the battleship itself, a group of Thraxian fighter pilots, and everyone inside the mining asteroid.

Z

Zenbat Oddnu IV - (Chapter 7) A planet located outside of the Galactic Government / Tiffan Siram Empire's jurisdiction.

Novelist Bio

Troy D. Wymer is a science fiction space opera novelist from Michigan, US. He started writing in 1984, but it wasn't until 2016 that he formed the WymerNovels imprint and began to publish novels. Troy enjoys reading, writing, and listening to various subgenres of metal music.